RACING HEARTS

Beth Smart

Fisher King Publishing

RACING HEARTS

Published by
Fisher King Publishing
The Studio
Arthington Lane
Pool in Wharfedale
LS21 1JZ
England
www.fisherkingpublishing.co.uk

To all the horses I have had the privilege of sharing my life with, I dedicate this book to you.

A great horse will change your life. The truly special ones define it.

This book is written in loving memory of my very own 'Iron Lady' Maggie.

My horse's feet are as swift as rolling thunder
He carries me away from all my fears
And when the world threatens to fall asunder
His mane is there to wipe away my tears.

Bonnie Lewis

Chapter One

I feel physically sick as I watch Dunkirk and Robbie canter to post. I know he isn't ready but as usual Lord Daventhorpe has got his way and threatened me with withdrawing his horses unless he is ready to win the Dante at York. I loathe the awful, stout, oversized tweed-suit wearing man and I always have since I was a little girl. He would always be there expressing his never-ending opinions; always right, jabbering on about his next attempt to conquer the world of racing and pressuring my father into running his horses everywhere and anywhere he deemed fit. That's what probably caused him to have a stroke which makes me loathe the man even more. To make matters worse my long-term boyfriend, the infamous Robert James, is his retained jockey so, in effect, I am encircled by the right honourable Lord Daventhorpe and his never-ending influence.

So, here I now stand, Emma Williams, daughter of the famed Richard Williams and walking target of Lord D as everyone seems to delight in calling the imbecile. Behind my designer pencil skirt and Dior heels, I am beginning to crack.

'And they're under starters orders… and they're off.' The

commentator's roaring voice rocks me out of my thoughts. The stalls fly open and the field surges forward. Dunkirk is quick to break, and Robbie eases him into 2nd place behind the frontrunner. My nausea intensifies, and tunnel vision overtakes me as I focus on the big screen. The racecourse is alive with activity only intensifying the nerves like electricity radiating through my stomach. The field races on into the turn. Dunkirk's easy stride eats up the ground and Robbie looks comfortable with his position and how the horse is going.

Robbie is such a poser sitting perfectly poised aboard Dunkirk looking around for challengers. I guess that's why I fell for him. He is always in control, perfect suit, perfect hair, says the right thing to those that matter. The field eat up the ground, Dunkirk, a gorgeous brown colt bred in the purple like all of Daventhorpe's horses, does not look out of place even though he is short of a few gallops, whether his blue blood will help us today is another matter. The other runners jostle for position behind him; this is sure to be a messy race for more reasons than one. I can barely breathe, my lungs feel full of concrete. I know Dunkirk isn't fit enough after his injury last year, yet here he is running in a Group 1 against some of the best horses from home and abroad. D-day has officially arrived. Ironic, I know. The field explodes into the home straight, oblivious to my inner turmoil. It is then that I know this is it, the beginning of the end, or you could say it had already begun with my father's illness and the impending doom of Lord Daventhorpe's wrath. Dunkirk drops back and Robbie begins to lay into him with his stick. They say if it looks ugly, it is ugly and this was definitely ugly.

'Robbie, give the horse a break.' I whisper. My heart drops into my stomach as Lord Daventhorpe begins to scream. 'Go on, go on, what's he doing I thought he would win.' His booming voice carries across the paddock where the connections have gathered to watch the big race. People turn to see where all the shouting is coming from. Embarrassed would be an understatement. His dark, heartless eyes bore into my inner soul from underneath the brown fedora that he insists on wearing everywhere; how I would like to flip it off his head and stamp on it. I try to ignore his chubby purple face; the race isn't over yet maybe by some miracle Dunkirk will sprout wings, turn into a unicorn or better still the ground will swallow me up. As the field nears the stands, the crowd erupts with whoops and hollers as the commentator shouts the winner in. Except it is not Dunkirk. Robbie has all but stopped riding and Dunkirk labours at the back of the field, making every stride seem like a marathon.

'This is ridiculous Emma. I stood by you after your father got sick, but this is it. It can't go on.' He states emphatically waving his arms in the air for effect.

'With respect, Sir, I told you he wasn't ready, but *you* insisted on running him.'

'Don't you dare try and shift the blame to me, I'm not the

one with the trainer's license.' He sneers, placing his hand on his chest for impact.

I cut him off. 'Which is why you should have listened to me when I told you he wasn't ready!' I feel like stamping my feet and screaming in his face. He acted like he was *never* wrong. Ever.

By this time, his attention has shifted to Robbie, who is approaching us aboard the heavily blowing Dunkirk, his sides heaving violently with each breath.

'He blew up, just wasn't fit, I'm sorry Em, you know it too.'

I shoot him daggers; if looks could kill, he'd be in the ground by now. I need him to be on my side for once instead of blowing smoke up Lord Daventhorpe's arse.

'Yes, as I thought,' he says contentiously, 'this horse needs a proper trainer.'

'Excuse me,' my voice rockets two octaves higher. I couldn't believe he was doing this right here in the middle of the parade ring loud enough for the whole racecourse to hear. 'That is very unfair and you know it.'

'I will not be questioned by a 21-year-old girl who's simply living off her father's reputation.'

Robbie has unsaddled by now and comes to my side adorned in Daventhorpe's all silver and gold striped colours, 'Steady sir she's trying her best.'

'Listen here Robert, if you want to keep your job, you will shut up and go and weigh in.' And that is it he just walks away from me, giving up when I need him most blending perfectly into the huddle of jockeys heading for the weighing room. We have drawn quite a crowd, including every media outlet of the racing world who are hanging off Lord Daventhorpe's every word.

'Make arrangements for the horses to be ready for transportation tomorrow morning.' Even though I knew it was coming, it is still like a punch in the stomach. My heart all but drops into the deep pits of my lungs, preventing all oxygen from getting in but I force my brain into forming a coherent sentence.

'With all due respect…' he cuts me off again.

'I don't need your opinion girl, just do it.' Completely speechless, I walk away from him, I have to, or I will do or say something I will live to regret. My legs carry me away from the vile man, and I simply let them. All the fight and enthusiasm I had as a teenager with bright horizons and dreams of a wonderful future have left me. The flood gates that I tried so desperately to keep shut open, so I let the hot, angry tears flow. I have been strong for so long, but I am tired of pretending. I head for Robbie's car ignoring everyone pushing through the throng of bodies and concerned and not so concerned racegoers enjoying the warm spring weather. One foot in front of the other. Nearly there… nearly there, I tell myself.

'Ooof.' I bump head-first straight into a very solid chest.

'Sorry,' I mumble and keep striding on not bothering

to look who it belongs to. I only make two strides when a strong hand wraps around my bicep.

'Are you ok?' A concerned male voice asks. I look up through my tear-stained vision into a pair of piercing blue eyes separated by a furrowed brow seemingly troubled by my state.

'Yes, thanks, sorry,' I mumble not stopping to take in any more of this person than absolutely necessary. I pull out of his hold, keeping my pace towards Robbie's jet-black Audi.

Eventually, Robbie makes his way out of the racecourse and strolls towards his car. He wears tight black jeans and a button-down shirt. He meets me with a sorry expression, bag slung over his shoulder, his blonde hair perfectly re-styled with that annoying parting I'd now come to hate, although I am yet to tell him. There is an awkward silence as neither of us knows who should speak first. He pops the boot and flings in his gear. I decide if he doesn't have the guts to address what has just happened, then I will have to speak first.

'He's taking the horses.'

'I know,' he replies.

'Is that all you have to say?'

'Don't be like that Em you knew it was inevitable.'

'Oh, and why's that?' I bite back.

'Listen Em, you're not your dad.' I can't believe what I am hearing, the one person who should stand by me through thick and thin is siding with the one person he knows I hate the most.

'And what's that supposed to mean?' I exclaim

'Please don't do this, let's not cause another scene Em, just get in the car, I'll take you home.'

How chivalrous. All the fight has left me, so I let Robbie take me home. The journey is painfully silent and lasts what feels like a lifetime. I want to be anywhere, with anyone that isn't here. To say this day has been a disaster would be the understatement of the century.

He pulls up in front of the trainer's house that represents my childhood home. He follows me out of the car and we stand in silence looking at each other, eyes locked in the middle of the yard with only Lord Daventhorpe's numerous horses for company. The stable lads must have left hours earlier.

'Look Em, I just don't think we're working. It hasn't been the same since your dad got sick.'

'Please don't do this,' I beg, my voice faltering as I speak, barely above a whisper. This is the last thing I need. I've already lost everything and everyone.

'You know it's the right thing for both of us.'

'The right thing? The right thing?' I screech with anger burning inside me. He can't meet my eyes; he won't look at me. What a coward he is, blaming this on my father when we both know it has everything to do with that insidious man Daventhorpe and Robbie's only love, riding winners. Trying to convince him that there is still an 'us' is futile, so I walk away, and he lets me. He *lets* me.

Chapter Two

I wake up early the next day, knowing sleep will only dull the pain for so long. I force myself to get up and to face the inevitable. Rays of sunlight force their way into my room with the hope of a new day, yet this day holds little to no hope, and the little hope I have has been evaporating with each second since I'd woken.

I pad into the bathroom to clean my teeth. I stare at my reflection in the mirror; I look horrific. I had gone straight to bed last night without showering or taking off my make-up. My curly strawberry blonde hair stands up in every direction and I look like I have two black eyes from crying. What has gone so horribly wrong? When did everything become such a mess? Why had dad got sick? Why is Daventhorpe such an awful man? If he could even be called a man. Had Robbie ever loved me? Obviously not, judging by how easily he let me go. At that realisation, tears threaten to fall again, gathering in hot pools behind my eyes. I angrily will them away; I will not start crying *again*. I decide to guard my heart closely; from this moment forward, I will never again let a man claim it and then cast it aside so easily. Jockeys are notorious for convenient relationships; I had thought that Robbie was different, that he truly reciprocated how I felt towards him, but it turns out he is just the same as the stereotype, small and disappointing. I take a quick shower and force some rationality to take residence in my over-active mind. I can do this. I can do this. I can do this. Can I do this?

I make my way downstairs where Sam is there to greet me, my pug best friend. I stand behind the locked door that leads to the yard, knowing that opening it will signal the reality of this day. A day that will bring the end of everything my dad has built. How I have disappointed him so much by letting it fall into such ruin. I brace myself and make my way outside. The atmosphere on the yard is tangible; it is obvious they all know of the impending moving of the horses. I will be left with three three-year-olds, Play Nicely, Silver Noble and Divine Right and Flashdance, a two-year-old unbroken colt by Galileo that my father had bred with Daventhorpe two years previously. He had been given to us after he had a diagnosis of angular limb deformity. Daventhorpe had wanted him put down as he put it, "it was not fit for purpose and would never win anything." I begged him to let me have him as I couldn't bear the thought of him being destroyed because Daventhorpe couldn't be bothered with the hassle. In the end, he told me to do what I want 'with it.' I really like the little horse, and I cling to the potential of what his breeding might bring. After him, there will be four broodmares Gaelic Blessing, Demelza, Divine Intervention who'd bred Divine Right and Iron Lady who is in foal. Their offspring's results have been good but nothing overly flash. Then there will be my old section B welsh pony, Gremlin, and who could race an elderly, fat pony? My life is officially a joke; I love him all the same though, he is a walking reminder of happier times.

'Go on, kick him on Emma,' dad shouts. My little legs barely reach the end of the saddle but they kick furiously encouraging Gremlin to canter faster, faster, faster up the hallowed turf.

'Yes that's it,' he laughs with elation. My cheeks can barely contain my smile; at this moment, I feel like a jockey, a real jockey, just like my dad.

As I make my way through the yard, the staff eye me warily. They all busy themselves with mucking out as usual. However, this is not a normal day. I ask them to gather around so I can explain the situation. They had all been very good to me after my father got sick and had kept working for me with very little questioning. The only one who had left was the stroppy assistant trainer, Ben, who had refused to 'serve under a girl' as he had put it. I had always thought he was a chauvinistic fool.

It takes a few minutes before they have all assembled, and I begin the unavoidable.

'I believe you are all aware of yesterday's events and as a result, Lord Daventhorpe has decided to withdraw his horses today.' I would have liked them to gasp or exclaim *oh no* or *I'm so sorry* but there is nothing but very loud silence. I continue anyway, 'so it goes without saying that the horses will not need exercising this morning but will have to be prepped to leave. I'm so sorry that it has come to this. Obviously, after the Daventhorpe horses leave, there will only be eight horses left. Which means, I won't be needing the full team of staff that we have now and for that, I'm truly sorry, I completely understand and would urge you all to find alternative employment. You will all be paid in full. Finally, I would like to thank you all from the bottom of my heart for sticking with me through all this. I know it hasn't been easy.' My voice breaks but by some miracle, I make it to the end of the sentence. A few of the lads give me their sympathies but the majority just slip off back into their morning duties. It is then that it hits me, they are only here because of my father's legacy, not silly little me just like Robbie had said. They probably never wanted me to take over, it was just easier to remain in their current jobs and with the Daventhorpe horses to ride there was obviously incentive to stay.

Damn, Robbie. I miss him already probably more than I should, I guess that's what happens when your first love deserts you on the same spot he'd picked you up for your first ever date.

'I promise I'll look after her sir.' Robbie said to my father who nodded his head and shot him a steely glare. Robbie looked so handsome in his light blue shirt, black trousers and brown loafers. His blonde hair was perfectly styled; his

intoxicating grey eyes never left me. My knees felt weak and my stomach flipped with butterflies. I couldn't believe the guy I'd had a crush on since the day he first stepped into our yard to ride work was actually taking me out. I just couldn't contain my smile.

'Since when did you start calling people sir?' I chuckled. He held out his hand for me and led me to the front of the trainer's house to his waiting Audi.

'Since I started taking out Richard Williams very beautiful daughter.' My cheeks blazed and he chuckled under his breath. He certainly knew how to make a girl swoon. I glanced back towards the house as Robbie opened the car door, my dad was watching us through one of the upstairs windows his brown-grey hair just visible in the evening light. I smiled to myself, ever the over-protective father.

He drove me to a gorgeous little Italian restaurant in nearby Wharton. Candles were the only lighting and romantic music set the atmosphere. The conversation flowed all night and he fed me compliment after compliment. At the end of the perfect first date, he drove me home. He ran around to the passenger side and opened the door for me. He walked me back into the yard with his hand placed lightly on the small of my back. We drew to a stop underneath the old oak that overlooked the yard. He turned me to face him and tucked a piece of my curly hair behind my ear. My heart beat so fast I thought the whole yard must be able to hear it. He gently gripped my chin between his thumb and his index finger so I was looking straight into his eyes. At that moment, time stood still. The world disappeared around us; we were the only two people who existed. We broke eye contact as his gaze swept lower towards my lips. He stepped a little closer and kissed me sweetly. His hands gently found my cheeks and I wrapped my arms around his neck. I was melting under his touch. After what felt like an eternity we broke apart and renewed our heated eye contact, his pupils had become dilated black pools. A horse in a nearby stable thrashed and we stepped apart. 'Thank you for tonight,' I said breathily.

'The pleasure was all mine.' I shivered as he graced me with that killer smile I'd come to love and with that, I was left standing in the yard with a goofy smile plastered all over my face.

Urgh, shut up brain. I do not need to do this to myself today of all days. Robbie will always hold a special place in my heart. After all, he was my first love, but I need to push him from my mind for now. Guard your heart remember.

The rumble of trucks and the smell of diesel brings me back to reality. Daventhorpe wasted no time. The horseboxes are those of a well-known transportation company. Daventhorpe isn't going to openly let me know where the horses are going by sending the trainer or trainers to collect them. I am not surprised though, the man has always been all smoke and mirrors. A short man with a balding head jumps out of the cab of the first lorry and limps over to greet me.

'Alright love?' I mean seriously? Does he want the truthful answer because the clean version would be absolutely not.

'Um…' It is going to be a big payday for him.

'Great, well let's get this show on the road lovey.' I meet him with a blank expression when really, I want to tell him to do one. *Show on the road,* come on I guess my life is turning into a bloody soap opera!

'Sarah,' I call to one of the grooms, 'bring him out first.'

And then it begins. Loading the horses is like a military operation. Blue-blooded thoroughbred after blue-blooded thoroughbred is led out of their stable and onto the waiting boxes. My father's legacy disappears one after another. Everyone seems so relaxed about the whole situation. Shit. They had been expecting this hadn't they, all of them - every single one. No one had expected me to be a successful trainer. They were just biding their time until they had to find other jobs. I feel so judged, so worthless, so used, so alone but most of all a complete failure.

By noon the yard is nearly empty, much like my heart and my head. The beautiful ancient yard hasn't been empty in hundreds of years and now it looks like an abandoned ghost town. All my emotions rush over me in a tsunami, the flood gates open once more and I just cry and cry and cry until my legs give way and I kneel on the hard, cold concrete as guttural sobs escape from my mouth. I am a failure, just a useless failure crying to myself alone in the middle of my now empty yard. I think back to something my dad used to tell me when I would cry down the phone from boarding school, 'nothing lasts forever petal.' How right he had been. Nothing, absolutely nothing lasts and I am alone once again.

All the staff have gone and honestly, I don't expect them back tonight or the next day. It is all on me now. It is a cold hard fact, I know this, yet I yearn for a friend or just someone to confide in; a comforting presence, anyone, anything. All my school friends had gone off to university to fulfil their bright futures and I had subsequently lost contact with them. They are having the times of their lives while here I am, standing in the middle of an abyss with nothing but a hungry pug for company.

Once I have cried all the water from my body, I peel myself off the now damp concrete and drag myself back into the trainer's house. I find the Racing Post placed on the kitchen table as it always had been when my father held the licence. My heart drops into my stomach as I recognise the heartbroken looking girl on the front cover standing next to Lord Daventhorpe.

Me.

The headline is just as bad as the photo of my tear-stained face splashed across the cover:

Lord D's defiance. Richard Williams' legacy not enough for daughter Emma as the honourable Lord Daventhorpe withdraws all his horses.

Lord Daventhorpe exclusively told the Racing Post that he

had stood by Emma Williams 'out of respect for her father' but has revealed that he considers her to be lacking in 'talent, experience and horsemanship.'

Horsemanship. Is he that deluded? The man doesn't know which end of a horse eats and which one shits!

Lord Daventhorpe's string of horses will now be trained by Ben Davies who spoke of his delight at receiving the call up after serving under William's father for many years. Robert James will remain in the coveted role of retained jockey; how that will affect his relationship with Emma Williams will remain to be seen.

I can't read the rest of the article. It is official everyone knows about my failings and when did the Racing Post turn into a gossip column talking about my relationship. Talk about adding insult to injury. I grab the paper and rip at it angrily. How dare he speak about my father. It is his fault he's in the state he is in and Ben, that son of a bitch, I bet he's been waiting for this all along.

…

I decide I need to go and visit my dad after all that has gone down even if he doesn't understand what is going on. I hop into my beaten-up old Golf and drive the half-hour trip to the home where he is cared for. I park up and make my way into the old country house. Surrounded by green fields, it is nice enough, but I long for him to be among the fields of home. I long for everything to go back to normal, long to see even a glimmer of my father that once was.

I stroll into reception to be greeted by the same preppy receptionist Joyce. 'Hello dear. How are you?' she nearly sing-songs.

'Been better thanks,' I reply quickly and maintain my pace to my father's room. If one more person today asks me if I'm alright I think I'll punch them. I know she's only being polite, but I am not in the mood for small talk. I'm not in the mood for much. I'd fed the horses a quick lunch before I left seeing as all of the staff had taken my 'urge' to find another job as gospel. Loyalty, what loyalty? No one even asked if I needed any help in any shape or form. I am my only family now.

I make my way upstairs to his room and knock softly on the door. There is no reply as usual, so I open the door quietly and make my way into the generic white space.

He sits limply in the same living room chair he sits in every day, staring without reason out of the window at the numerous sheep that graze the surrounding area. His grey hair is neatly trimmed but his skin is an icky grey colour. He doesn't live anymore; he just exists in this one room with only an occasional nurse for company.

'Hi daddy,' I whisper. He is only the shell of the man I once knew. The all-knowing, opinionated, successful trainer is long gone. He smiles up at me and even though that should cheer me up, it only makes hot tears line my eyes. I angrily will them away; I will not cry in front of him. I won't. I can't, not today.

I need to admit to him what has happened even if he doesn't understand. 'I've let you down, I'm so sorry. I wish I could change things,' I mutter. He just keeps smiling at me with only love in his eyes.

'Where did you go daddy? You must be in there somewhere?' A tear escapes down my cheek. I quickly go to swipe it away but instead, he places his wrinkly wizened hand over mine. The comfort he offers me breaks my heart a little more; it is the best he can do with the body that has so cruelly failed him. After my mumbled confession, I sit with him for the next hour thanking God that he is still here with me since everyone else seems to have left, even if he can't speak.

We sit in the quiet watching the world go by. Even though I should be comforting him, it is him that makes the pain ease just a little bit. Even my mum upped and left years ago after she had a massive argument with my dad over Daventhorpe and some scheme he'd cooked up in which my dad had been implicated. She'd said goodbye and sorry to me, then left. She wouldn't explain, and she wouldn't let me convince her to stay. I was so hurt that the woman who'd brought me into this world could just up and leave like that. It was a horrible reality to face at only twelve years old. She was gone in a flash never to return. She made it clear she wanted to be as far away from us as possible when she boarded that plane to America. She now has a new boyfriend called Hunter. I mean come on, who's even called that? She doesn't answer my calls even after all these years, all that's left of her is the colour of my hair, the only thing she'd been so kind as to leave me with.

No-one ever told me fully what had gone on, so I just carried on with my life. I would always hear that I didn't need to worry 'my pretty little head.' Losing my mother like that had been tough but she'd always been quite hands-off. I was packed off to boarding school as soon as physically possible, fed the line that 'it would be *good* for me'. Honestly now I look back she was only happy when she was being photographed in the winner's enclosure of some prestigious racecourse. As soon as things got rough, she was gone.

A nurse with brown hair and a kind face, dressed in a tailored white uniform, enters the room to check on my father. I am aware that that is my signal to depart, so I kiss him gently on the cheek and take my leave. Our eyes meet for the briefest moment as I go; it breaks my heart once again to see him like this. Alive but at the same time so lifeless.

The drive home is quick and before I know it, I am back at the empty yard. It is like a ghost town. I let Sam out and he follows me as I muck out and feed the horses. The broodmares are down in the paddocks so I move the three-year-olds and Flashdance into the barn so they can be close together. They greet me with their heads over the stable doors with the white blaze of Flashdance standing out on his pretty bay face. I always feed Flash first as he gets narky if I don't. I think he knows his father is a champion and by paternal rights, he should always get extra attention. He eats too fast and gets some chaff up his nose then sneezes all over me. I laugh for the first time in weeks at his confused expression. He'd always been a character even when dad and I would go and see him at the vet's, he would always have a cheerful outlook on life.

I feed the other horses and check the broodmares in the fields who graze happily. I inhale the fresh evening air to try and centre myself. I haven't spoken to Robbie since yesterday and the fateful day of the Dante. I guess he is showing me his true colours. He hasn't even texted me to see how I am. A pang of what I think is jealousy washes over me as I picture him moving on with some glamorous girl. I am definitely not that girl, what with my curly red hair and petite frame. Being dumped is not recommended, it feels like crap, especially given the pathetic excuse he had fed me. I mean seriously, he might as well have done it by text.

I drag myself back to the house, the events of the last day catching up with me all at once. I feel so alone. I rattle around in all the rooms of the trainer's house; it is a house meant for people. I still sleep in my childhood room although the décor has been radically overhauled from the purple ponies and posters of *Mcfly. Don't judge ok.* Robbie had stayed with me after my father got sick, but as soon as the results began to lapse, he would spend less time with me and would make excuses instead. *Liar.*

I slump into the old leather sofa in the living room and

Sam hops onto my lap and snuggles down. I stroke his fawn coat, it is just Sam and me and the memories of a time gone by displayed by the countless winner's photos hanging on every wall. I gaze around at them one by one, above the fireplace hangs Thatcher's Girl, One Thousand Guineas winner and Iron Lady's dam. Next to her hangs Lady Daventhorpe winning the Oaks for Robbie, Daventhorpe and my dad, that was his proudest moment, I smile to myself. One of the biggest photos in the room hangs next to the door, Priory Castle winning the King George Stakes at Glorious Goodwood. Named after Daventhorpe's estate, he was one of the best horses Daventhorpe ever owned. Robbie gave him a perfectly timed ride that day, one of his best, even by my own admission. It had always been a mystery to me why Daventhorpe sold him to Australia after he won. It's not as if he needed the money and dad was lining him up for the Nunthorpe at Daventhorpe's favourite track York.

My perusal around the living room makes me even more angry at him; how he could ever hold anything over my dad is a mystery to me. He doesn't owe him anything; he'd trained him countless winners and given Daventhorpe the prestige he so desperately craved.

'I guess we'll never know Sammy.' I smile down at my little pug who snores oblivious to my ramblings. 'Time to sleep methinks.' I lift him onto the ground and he looks up at me in disgust as I trudge up to bed.

Chapter Three

A week later, I stare at my bank account on the computer screen willing some zeros to appear but to no avail. Daventhorpe has paid up until last month, but I am resigned to the fact that I probably won't be seeing the remaining fees. Daventhorpe never does anything he doesn't want to. There is no way I can live off this for the rest of my life now that no training fees are coming in. I go through all the possibilities of raising much-needed funds; rob a bank, steal one of Daventhorpe's prize paintings, get my old job at the *Winning Post* back. But realistically the answer is staring me in the face; Do I have the heart to sell one of my father's prized mares? Iron Lady is in foal to Dark Angel and is a half-sister to Group winning sprinter Priory Castle and could make decent money at the sales while Demelza has bred four winners. I weigh up the pros and cons. Selling one of them would give me the much-needed cash to keep the yard going, but I don't know if my heart will let me whatever my brain says. The staff need to be paid. I don't have the heart to sell Iron Lady's unborn foal as well so it will have to be Demelza. *God, this is horrible.*

A wave of pragmatism washes over me and I check to

see when the next mare sales are to be held. Next week, and there are still places available. I call the sales company and they willingly agree to auction Demelza on my behalf. How gracious I think sarcastically. I feel awful but it has to be done.

The monotone auctioneering makes my skin prickle as the sale begins. The sound invades the sales complex; there is no escape from it. It always sickened my stomach even when I'd come to the sales as a child. The bidding battles which ensue over and over again disturb me as it so clearly demonstrates what money wants, money gets. Money, money, money. Money makes the world go around or is it love? Don't get me wrong I never wanted for anything as a child, but here the amount of money exchanged for one living breathing single horse was obscene.

I arrive early to avoid too much attention; however, my flying under the radar is short-lived. Viewing after viewing ensues. It is nearly time for me to take Demelza up to the ring when a short, skinny man with a sheet white face sidles up to me, his energy immediately putting me on edge.

'Can I see her out Miss?' His tinny voice reverberates around my skull. I reluctantly pick up Demelza's bridle and place it gently on her petite chestnut head. I hate this, to say I feel terrible is the understatement of the century. The man watches me with intent as I pull her out of the stable after picking out and greasing her feet. I lead her up the yard so he can see her gait. I would like to just keep walking. I reluctantly turn and lead Demelza back towards him. I stand her up with all four limbs showing so he can inspect her. His prying eyes run over her briefly, but it is clear I am the specimen he is more interested in examining. It makes the hair on my bare arms stand on end.

'So,' he starts, 'what's she bred?'

'I believe all her offspring and their results are listed in your catalogue sir,' I speak sweetly with a fake smile plastered on my face.

'Yes, yes.' *Weirdo.* 'How's your dear father these days?'

'He's well,' I reply shortly not wanting to go down this route of conversation.

'Things have gone downhill for you, haven't they?'

My resolve snaps. 'Look I have no idea who you are or what paper you work for, but unless you are interested in purchasing, I suggest you take your questions elsewhere.' His face never alters, he simply continues to stare right at me, raking his eyes up and down my body. I turn to lead the mare back into her stable when he finally speaks.

'Just trying to do my job dear. My readers would be very interested in what you have to say.'

Urgh. What a slimy man. *Dear. I mean, seriously, who does he think he is?* With a deathly stare and a swish of my hips, I lead Demelza back into the stable while he stalks off back into the crowded sales yards.

The time has come for me to take Demelza up to the parade ring. I look into her perfect brown eyes my resolve beginning to snap. I love her like a human being. Her gorgeous eyes never leave mine; she is so noble in all this. It is as if she knows what she has to do. Looking into each other's eyes, we can see straight into one another's soul. She knows it is time, so I lead her out of the haven of the quiet stable and up to the ring.

She has been popular in the yards with multiple viewings but I feel like people are more interested in gawking at me than actually showing a direct interest in viewing the mare. The lot before has just sold, so I lead Demelza into the ring. Many agents strut in behind us. In one way I hope she'll be popular and sell well but the other side of me hopes that she doesn't sell and I can take her home, put her back in the field and find another few zeros added to the bank. The striking up of the bidding puts those thoughts to bed. Agents lean over the rails like macho men at a boxing match; they elbow each other for space, making me feel like the walls are closing in. I keep my head down and concentrate on leading Demelza around the ring.

'And its ten bid, ten bid now,' the auctioneer drones on trying to incite a frenzy of bidding. Another bid goes in, 'and it's 20,000, 20,000 now. Someone give me twenty-five now. Bred by the great Richard Williams. A dam of multiple winners and a daughter of the great Danehill.' At that moment, I feel a pang of anger towards my father. Why does he have to be a multiple classic winning trainer? Why am I falling so short of fulfilling his legacy? Why am I doing this?

I stamp those feelings down. It isn't his fault, it is all mine.

The bidding goes on and then stalls at 24,000, a respectable price. But it is then that I see him. That man. That insidious man Daventhorpe. He raises his hand and bids 30,000. The ring falls silent. The agents stop their antics and close their catalogues. What does he want now? I look up into the rafters of the ring. There he is in that hideous tweed suit and that god-damn awful hat. He won't meet my gaze; he simply holds the auctioneer with those piercing dark eyes. He's already ruined my life enough. No one dares even to lift a finger once they know Daventhorpe is in the bidding. The auctioneer wraps up the sale and bangs his hammer onto the hardwood of his rostrum, 'Sold! Lord Daventhorpe, a good buy sir.'

I lead her out of the ring slightly breathless from the roller coaster of emotions I'd felt in there. Daventhorpe slithers over to me and taps me on the shoulder. 'Bernice can take it from here,' he slurs. I look up to see a short middle-aged woman with greying hair appear from behind him to take Demelza from me. She yanks the lead rope from my hands and leads Demelza into the maze of the sales complex. He hasn't even given me the chance to say goodbye. Sadness quickly turns to anger 'Are you going to pay me now Sir? I ask sarcastically.

'You may not address me in public,' he sneers.

I have no words - none. People gather around congratulating him and telling him how gracious he is to support a struggling trainer. I stand there gawking like an imbecile. *You may not address me in public.* What the hell? I can't stand this any longer. I will not be a circus act for Daventhorpe to conduct as he pleases. This trainer wouldn't be struggling if it wasn't for him.

I spin on my heel and head for the horsebox. I can't breathe, the air is suffocating and hot-angry tears fall down my already tear-stained face. I push past people who wind me when they don't move. I walk as quickly as I can amid the throng, my legs not carrying me fast enough, tears are blurring my vision. Why am I crying again? It is a miracle I still have any water left in my body but I have been strong for too long. Too long I have held it in. Suddenly my foot gets caught and I fall face-first into the dirty gravel. I hit the ground with such a thud that the air is forced out of my lungs. The chalky chippings scratch the skin of my hands and knees and the taste of blood spills into my mouth. I must have bitten my lip on impact. I stay there splayed in the dirt; no-one tries to help me. It feels like a replay of the Good Samaritan except my Samaritan is delayed on the way to Jericho. Slimy journalist man from earlier appears taking photos of me lying in the dirt.

'What would you like to say about the withdrawal of Lord Daventhorpe's horses now? Are you happy he bought your father's mare? Who's taking their questions elsewhere now, *dear girl*?' Upon his insistent questioning my resolve crumbles and the tears come faster and the taste of blood unrelenting.

'Hey, leave her alone,' a lone voice shouts. I heave my head up to be greeted by a familiar pair of blue eyes. He kneels beside me and asks in hushed worried tones, 'Are you ok? Are you hurt?' He places his hand on my shoulder, and I look up into his ocean-like eyes. The tears are relentless. I can't seem to form a coherent sentence. He gently wraps his hand around my arm and pulls me into a sitting position. I continue to cry silently. I love that mare and now I am unlikely ever to see her again. I'd known that when I decided she had to be sold but why to Lord Daventhorpe? He scans my battered body up and down, noticing the wounds to my hands and my continuous stream of tears.

'It's ok; I'm here, I'll help you.' His kindness only makes me feel more upset. He looks so concerned for me. Me, a stranger he'd never met sitting in the middle of a dirty sales complex with blood everywhere. 'Here,' he offers me his hand, 'let me help you get cleaned up. I'm Tom by the way.' My fight or flight mechanism has gone along with all of my vocabulary, so I place my bloodied palm into the warmth of his hand as he gently helps me to my feet.

I expect him to pull his hand from mine as soon as I am upright, but he keeps it there. I should pull away but he makes me feel safe and not alone for the first time in ages. After a few unsteady strides, he places an arm around my waist to support my weight. We walk in contemplative silence, his hand never leaving mine even though it would probably have blood smeared all over it by now. He leads me into the stable lad's canteen and asks for a first aid kit. Upon seeing my sorry outline, the dinner lady gladly obliges. The few lads in there look up from their gravy clad meals to gawk for a second but I am thankful that they seem more interested in their food than me, which makes a change. I am fed up with being the centre of everyone's whispered conversations.

He pulls out a chair for me. 'Here, take a seat,' he gestures. He pulls out another chair directly opposite and sits down so that our knees are nearly touching. He sets the first aid box on the table, takes out a wipe and gently dabs at my wounded hands. It is then that I can take him in. He is beautiful, warm blue eyes, dark brown hair, muscular, he definitely works out, but with his good looks, an aura of kindness seeps from his very being.

My crying fit begins to subside but tears still leak out of the corners of my eyes.

'I'm so sorry about this.' His head snaps up from cleaning my hands,

'Hey, hey,' his hand finds my shoulder, 'don't cry. None of this is your fault,' he looks at me with eyes filled with sincerity.

'I'm Emma,' I offer out of politeness.

'I know,' he replies, offering me a lopsided smile. 'I think we already met.'

'Oh yeah right,' I mumble, 'York.'

'York indeed,' he nods.

'For what it's worth,' he offers, 'Daventhorpe's a complete crook.'

'Thanks,' I reply, 'I guess you and me both agree on that one.' He pulls out a bandage from the box and gently wraps it around my hands. My heart is beating out of my chest. I tell myself that it is just the shock. He finishes wrapping my hands then looks to my knees.

'I think you're going to need some new jeans.' I look down examining my knees properly for the first time. It is a sorry sight, blood mixed with gravel, denim and horse crap. Lovely.

'Oh gosh, well as they've ripped, I'll be extra fashionable now,' I say with a faint laugh.

'Put em in the wash, they'll be grand,' he chuckles.

'You're Irish,' I exclaim dumbly. He meets me with a lopsided smile.

'I am, although you can't always tell, I've been living in the US so I sound a lot more English these days.' Seeing as my jeans have ripped, he easily cleans up my knees and gently places plasters on them.

'Thank you so much. I really mean it, it's been a while since someone's helped me out so thanks.' I offer a weak smile. He is still observing me closely with those hypnotising eyes, dark features and dark brown hair. We stand up in unison, cross the canteen to the door and side by side step back into the yard.

'So, what brings you to the sales?'

'My parents have a small stud back home in Ireland. They asked me to come and view some mares that they were interested in.'

'Buy anything?

'No, not today. I loved your mare though.' I don't know what to say, it physically hurts to address Demelza in the past tense. He notices I've stiffened up, 'sorry, too soon,' he says with a tinge of regret.

'No, it's fine. Don't worry about it; it's not your fault. You're the only person who's been remotely nice to me in ages so please don't apologise.' I stare up at him to try and judge his reaction, but he continues to study me intently.

'Why?'

'Why what?' I ask stumped.

'Why is no one *remotely nice to you,*' he quotes. I flush a little at his interrogation.

'People change, things change, people leave.'

'Mmmhmm.' He is clearly thinking something that I can't decipher. We reach Demelza's designated stable and I gather up my stuff as he picks up my grooming kit.

'You don't have to do that.'

'I want to,' he replies with sincerity. I set off for the box. I need to get home to feed the horses seeing as there would be no one to do it for me.

'So, are you going back to Ireland tonight,' I ask.

'No,' he responds, 'only my parents and my sister lives there now.'

'So where do you live?'

'Well, I've just got back from the US. I've been riding out there for a few years. I'm staying with some old mates.'

'How come?' I ask. He stiffens slightly, 'sorry, I'm being nosy.'

'No, not at all. It's just… a long story.' We reach the box signalling the time has come for us to part company. He looks at me and my heart speeds up, still shocked, I tell myself.

I turn to face him as he hands me my kit. 'Thank you; I truly mean that.'

'It was nothing, good luck with everything.' He replies, holding me with that signature stare to which I was now getting accustomed. I pull open the door and hop in the cab.

'Thank you again.' He nods and closes the door for me, and I begin the long journey home.

Chapter Four

I wake the next morning to the sound of rain hammering on the windows and wish sleep to take me back but unfortunately, that isn't an option. I toss the covers aside, get up, get dressed and make my way downstairs. I pause in the kitchen, savouring the warmth of the Aga. As I approach the door, the rain is still battering the yard. That's what you get for training in the middle of the Yorkshire Moors. I sort through the old coats and rugs and find some waterproofs. The slightly stale smell of musty clothing and blankets invade my senses. I reluctantly make my way to unlock the door, Sam pushes past me into the yard and is soaked in seconds. His fawn coat now brown with all the water it is holding.

'Look at you, you silly thing.' I call into the rain as he spins around chasing his tail.

I force myself out of the house and make a dash to the American barn glad that the horses aren't stabled in the main yard. I heave open the sliding door and that heavenly smell of horse rolls into my nostrils as I take a deep breath. I am greeted with a chorus of nickers and snuffles although it is mainly Gremlin disgusted that I am at least one minute late serving his breakfast. He was called Gremlin for a reason. He swishes his liver chestnut mane and pokes his pink nose just high enough so he can see over the stall door and so that I can make out his big white face. I pull out a rounded scoop of nuts for Flash who greets me as always with his majestic brown face and white blaze. I then make my way down the line, first is the strapping grey Silver Noble, next to him is the almost black Play Nicely and then the pretty all bay mare Divine Right. Then I set about mucking out. When we'd had an army of staff, I hadn't needed to muck out, but I'd always enjoyed it. Shovelling poo brought a sense of peace to the soul. Sam seems to be enjoying his foray into the world of horse poo, snuffling down mouthfuls of it. At the sight of him taking mouthful after mouthful with a look of great delight on his face, I make a mental note to feed him less breakfast. Gross.

'Hey, stop that!' I chuckle.

It doesn't take long to muck out the five stables as the broodmares are still out in the fields. Iron Lady is in foal to Dark Angel which is exciting yet scary as I haven't foaled a mare before, realistically I need some help on that front. I file that thought for later and head for the tack room, the rain still pelting the yard. These horses need riding if I am ever going to run them and earn some money or better still attract some new owners. Flash will also need backing at some point.

The smell of leather brings a smile to my face; there

is nothing better than the hope and promise of a full tack room. My exercise saddle and bridle sit in pride of place on my peg however they haven't been touched for months as I stopped riding out to concentrate on training. I haven't had the time or the money to change the exercise sheets, they are still adorned with my father's initials, RDW. I feel a pang of sadness in the pit of my stomach. The yard should be bustling with activity yet here I am, alone in the middle of a fully stocked tack room staring at a pile of navy and red exercise sheets gathering dust. I pull myself together, angry at my thoughts, put on my boots, grab my hat and body protector and walk out of the tack room with a new purposeful determination. I decide to ride Divine Right first; the bay filly had always been very sweet and never seemed to give the lads much bother on the gallops although she will be fresh after nearly a week off. Fun! I tack her up quickly and pull her out of the stable, all the while Flash watching us intently.

'This will be you soon pretty boy,' I tell him while he looks at me questioningly. I laugh to myself and lead the filly to the end of the barn. It is still raining, lovely. I really need someone to leg me up but there is no one so I lead her to the indoor school. She fidgets around the mounting-block but eventually I mount without too much fuss. I give her a trot in the school to get the freshness out of her before I take her up the gallops plus I want to avoid getting anymore drenched than I otherwise might if I use the outdoor trotting ring. I ask her to trot on with a light aid and she gladly obliges, happy to be in work. She moves freely around the school with a spring in her step. The small break has done her good. After about ten minutes, I decide to brave the gallops. It has been a while since I've been up there and my fitness has significantly waned. As I come out of the school, a pheasant flies out in front of us, the filly veers violently to the side and I lose my stirrup.

'Whoa, there girl,' I soothe and give her a light pat on the neck.

My heart is beating significantly faster now, blood rushing in my ears. Calm down, I tell myself. I can do this. I give her another quick pat to calm myself more than her and steer her towards the woodchip of the gallops where I kick her on. As soon as her feet meet the woodchip Divine Right starts to jig-jog and takes hold of the bit pulling at my shoulders.

'Steady filly.'

I let my body weight shift forward to allow her to canter on. She takes a keen hold and I sit against her using the double bridge in my reins for security. I feel the rise and fall of her ribcage against my legs as she tugs me around the bend and up the straight of the gallops. Her feet hit the ground in perfect rhythm, her small dished face moving up and down to meet me with each stride. Whoever said that when you ride a horse you borrow freedom was absolutely right. There is no feeling like it in the whole universe. An engine could never replace the flesh and blood of the thoroughbred. The top is in sight, my shoulders and legs burn, and the rain blurs my vision. I am not riding fit. I begin to pull back slightly to ask her to steady, she tugs the bit back and for a moment my sticky reins, not helping matters, slip. Just when I think she is going to career into the fence at the top, she eventually comes back into a hack canter, trot and then walk.

She is blowing heavily once she pulls up, nearly as much as me. I am officially freezing, the rain and the cold wind has burnt my cheeks and I am soaked through to my underwear despite the fact I am wearing waterproofs. As we walk home, I survey the landscape I've come to call my own now that it is my name on the deeds. The rolling hills, the dry-stone walls. I wonder about the many horses that have graced this land in the hundreds of years it has been a racing establishment. Many a classic winner has exercised on this hallowed turf including a Derby winner trained by the late great Thomas London who'd sold the land and the yard to my father many years ago. Who'd have thought that after hundreds of years of rich racing history this small landscape in Yorkshire was now in the care of little old me?

We walk home nice and quiet until I hop off to walk back into the yard. She starts sidestepping away from me. My hands slither on the slippery orange rubber of the reins and I can barely keep hold of her. 'Maybe I should enter you up,' I voice, 'I'll send you up again if you're not careful Mrs,' I warn. I need someone to ride out with me, especially if something happens. I cool her off, untack her, give her some more haylage and make my way into the house for breakfast. I fix myself a coffee, sit down at the large oak table and pull out my battered I-phone. Even though the money from the sale of Demelza has come into my bank account, my troubles aren't going to disappear that easily. I have to continue to feed the horses, plus the care fees for my dad are not cheap. I call my old boss to see if there are any free shifts at the Winning Post, the pub where I worked as a teenager.

'Emma, honey, how are you?' chimes Clare the Winning Post's landlady.

'I'm ok thanks, Clare. How are things with you?' I hesitate, a sudden wave of butterflies settling in my stomach, 'I was wondering if any free shifts are going at the pub?' I ask tentatively.

She pauses for a second; I think she is going to point-blank refuse.

'Of course honey. You've always worked hard. We're actually short of someone tonight if you're free?' I let out a heavy breath I didn't know I'd been holding.

'Yes, yes I'm free, thank you Clare, I'll see you later, thank you.' I hang up before she can change her mind.

...

Later that evening, as I drive the short distance to the pub, I am overtaken with nerves and a sick feeling in my stomach. The Winning Post is *the* racing pub where everyone who is anyone congregates after evening stables whether you are a stable lad out for a quick pint or a trainer taking owners to eat in the restaurant. I dread seeing the racing circle there, but I *need* a job and Clare is a great boss.

I pull up underneath the huge winning post replica at the front of the old-white pub, hop out and lock my poor beat-up Golf. I heave open the oak panelled door. Even though it is only six in the evening, the pub is already busy. The *Winning Post* is a traditional Yorkshire pub with oak panelling around the walls and beams running across the ceiling. The influence of racing is everywhere, colours hanging in frames adorn the walls along with pictures of famous Yorkshire horses winning at the likes of Royal Ascot. My father's navy colours with red braces hang proudly on the back wall. I am filled with a rush of pride.

When people realise who has just entered, they all turn to look at me, *correction,* inspect me. Deathly silence ensues. I feel a hot blush breaking out across my cheeks and down my neck as I register the number of eyes boring into me. The silence is broken when a stable lad in the back knocks over his pint. Upon his drunken laughter, normal service is resumed. I make my way further through the pub and out of the doorway with my head held high. These judgemental bigots would not cow me. I find Clare behind the bar, her blonde, slightly greying hair flowing around her shoulders. She is a tall, slightly rotund lady; her upbeat personality spreads joy everywhere she goes. The *Winning Post* is her and her husband Chris' life.

'Emma honey, you're just in time.'

'Thank you so much for having me.'

'Oh, come here honey, give me a hug.' She envelops me in a glorious bear hug, 'You've turned into such a beautiful young woman.' I blush slightly at her remark but her show of endearment gives me a warm fuzzy feeling in my chest that I haven't felt in so long.

'Aw thank you Clare, I've missed this place. Where would you like me tonight?'

'Behind the bar would be great lovely. I've got to go and see to the B and B upstairs. Chris is in the kitchen if you need anything.'

I pull on a pinny and wash my hands in the sink. The place is filling up quickly and it isn't long before the orders start to come thick and fast. People lean across the bar ordering their drinks and food. It is just me serving, Clare wasn't kidding when she said that they were short tonight. I get back into the groove of bartending fairly quickly, as a teenager I could pull pints with my eyes closed. I am just taking a food order when a gnarly voice slurs, 'Pint, please darlin.' I turn around to find a thirty-something skinny guy with greasy black hair and a wrinkled brow.

'One second, just let me take this to the kitchen.' He looks completely disgusted at my reply so I scuttle away before he can make a come-back. In the seconds it takes me to run to the kitchen and back, his expression has significantly darkened.

'Ok, sorry, what can I get you?' I pant.

'I just told you,' he sneers openly staring at my chest. *Not cool.*

'Right a pint, sorry,' I rush flustered. I pull his pint willing the bitter liquid to flow from the tap as quickly as possible so I can get away from him. I go to place his pint lightly on the bar, but he rips it roughly from my grasp, some of it spilling onto my hands, and onto the coins he'd dropped onto the wood. I wrinkle my nose; beer was not my favourite thing. He slopes into the back of the pub to join what looks like his friends.

'Damn, I hope everyone's not like that around here,' says a familiar girly voice. I spin around to find my best friend from boarding school, Liv Mathews. She's hardly changed, her signature wavy blonde hair still hanging freely around her shoulders. I lean across the bar to hug her.

'Oh my gosh Liv, I've missed you so much!'

'Emma where've you been hiding, it's like you disappeared into thin air and then I saw you on the front of the Racing Post last week.' I chuckle, she hasn't changed one bit.

'Um, yeah.' I mumble. When my dad got sick and I took over the yard, I didn't think about anything other than training the horses. I feel bad; we had been so close as teenagers. I fill her in on everything that has gone down since she left to go to university.

'Oh that is awful Emmy, I'm so sorry.' She looks at me forlornly. I hate it when people give me that look.

'Don't look at me like that.' I scold.

'Sorry sorry sorry. I just wish you'd called.'

I feel terrible, we'd been so close at school, practically inseparable even though we are polar opposites. She is outgoing, a fashionista and is super modelesque gorgeous. I, on the other hand, am more of an introvert who prefers my Ariats to heels and is having a bad hair life, not just a day. However, we are united in our love of horses. Where I was always destined to follow in my father's footsteps, Liv loved her showjumping. Either way, we had always been horse mad ever since the days of hobby horses and *Breyer* models.

'I know, I'm sorry too. So, tell me, what have you been up to and what on earth are you doing here?'

'I graduated from Liverpool last year. Now I am an associate in York, but I've just rented a house in Wharton.'

'I can't believe you're here. I feel quite emotional.' I actually feel choked up. I am definitely in need of human contact.

'Calm down, you're going to make me cry.' She swats my arm and then we're laughing.

At this point, the greasy guy returns.

'Pint,' he states gruffly. I meet Liv with knowing eye contact; we have always been able to tell what each other is thinking, including silently judging people. I set about pulling his pint while he surveys Liv up and down.

'Dude, not cool,' she retorts. He grunts. What a lovely man. Please come again. Not! He pays and shuffles off to the back once again.

'Well, he was ew.' Liv whispers. 'Anyway,' she speaks up, 'how's that jockey you were gushing over when we last spoke?' My face falls and being my best friend, she notices immediately.

'Jerk!' she exclaims. 'Urgh, knew it.'

I go over the events of the last few months of our relationship. How Robbie had been supportive to start with but had grown increasingly distant. Then how he'd dumped me without as much as a second thought. It hurt bad but having Liv here made me feel much better.

'That is shitty. You have my number, right? If you want to talk just shout.' I nod. 'Well don't fear because there's a really hot guy checking you out over there.' I give her a yeah right look.

'I'm serious,' her voice rises an octave. 'Don't look now.' I spin on my heal to find familiar deep blue eyes studying the back of my head. Tom.

'Too late,' she chuckles as I begin to gape at him.

'Tom, hi!' I blush, somehow he has an effect on me.

'Emma,' he sounds pleased. He strolls over to stand opposite me beside Liv, who is giving me wide eyes with a smirk on her face.

'This is Liv,' I supply, eyeing my best friend.

'Nice to meet you,' they shake hands. Liv winks at me; it is obvious she can see that he affects me. His gorgeousness cannot go unnoticed. I pull myself together, the only times we'd met so far I'd either been crying, mute or both. Not my most attractive qualities.

'What are you doing here? Sorry,' I correct, 'can I get you anything?' He smiles wide at my awkward babble.

'A pint would be great thanks.' I set about fixing his pint while he and Liv made aimless small talk. Our hands brush as I hand him his pint and he pulls out some change. My heart lurches revelling in his warm touch.

'So, what brings you to the Winning Post,' Liv cuts in, in tune with my apparent loss of words.

'I'm just visiting an old friend in Wharton while I look for a job.' An unfamiliar ring tone sounds out and Liv digs her phone from her bag.

'Sorry, be back in a minute.'

'You need a job?' I cut in.

'Yeah, I only arrived back in the UK last week, so only just started looking.'

'I could really use some help. I mean that's if it's what you want. I know it's not much, I can't pay a lot, but I really could use a hand and thank you for the other day it meant a lot.'

I draw breath, wow I really need to shut up. Tom smiles and chuckles, apparently, my verbal diarrhoea is amusing.

'Emma...' wow my name sounds the best it's ever sounded coming from his mouth, 'it was nothing, and if you're sure.'

'I'm sure if you're sure. So are you staying here tonight?

I know you said you were staying with an old friend. Sorry, am I being nosy again?'

'Do you do that a lot?' he sounds amused.

'What?' I ask confused

'Ramble.'

'Oh, um yeah, I guess.'

'It's kind of adorable.' Adorable. Did he just call me adorable? 'And to answer your question, yes I am until I can work something out.'

'You can come and stay on the yard. Honestly, I haven't been into the staff cottages in a while so who knows what state they're in, but you don't look like a psychopath. You wouldn't have to pay rent or anything; you're doing a massive favour coming to help me out.' He looks at me, obviously amused. 'I'm rambling again, aren't I?'

'Something like that but seriously if you're sure, that would be great. To be honest, I hadn't thought about where I was going to live or anything.'

'Well, it's settled, you can live on the yard. You can come tonight if you want.' On cue, Clare arrives back down the stairs from the B and B.

'Who is this lovely young man Emma? I feel like I recognise him from somewhere.' Tom goes a little tense at her interrogation.

'This is Tom, he's coming to work for me starting tomorrow.' I look to him for confirmation. He is studying me intently.

'Emma here needs a nice young man in her life. That Robert was a stuck-up twat.'

'Clare!' I exclaim completely embarrassed, turning beet red at the same time. I have never heard her address anyone like that before. It is weird hearing something like it come out of her mouth but funny, nonetheless.

'Oh lovely girl I feel like a mother to you and in my opinion, he was never going to be the one.'

By this time Liv has returned from her phone call and is nearly wetting herself laughing. Tom continues to study the situation with amusement, those blue eyes never seeming to leave me.

'Put it there,' Liv exclaims holding her hand up for Clare to high five which she returns gladly.

It is getting late and people are beginning to head home ready for early morning stables tomorrow.

'Emma dear, if you clean down the bar you can head out for the night,' says Clare leaving to help Chris finish up in the kitchen. I set about wiping up the bar as greasy guy returns yet again. He plonks his sticky pint glass on the bar, burps and sways his way out of the pub.

'Well he was just delightful,' exclaims a rather aghast Liv. 'I'll get you his number if you want. You would look cute together. Opposites and all.' I laugh and bat my arm at her, how I missed this crazy girl.

'You're a bit crazy.' Chimes Tom turning to Liv. He hasn't stopped watching me from the moment he'd entered the pub. If he weren't so gorgeous, I would call him out on it.

'And I'm sober right now,' winks Liv while punching Tom on the arm. I give her a look, she is seriously going to scare him away if we aren't careful. 'Anyways I better be going, I only came down here for a look-see. Do you have a twin?' she asks Tom seriously, who is starting to look a little uncomfortable.

'Um, no, sorry.' I give her another look.

'Okay, okay, I'm going. It was lovely to meet you,' she says pointedly to Tom, 'and you ring me any time, any hour, I'm here for you. I mean it,' she says, leaning over to hug me.

'Thanks, I will, I promise.'

'You better,' she shouts as she makes her way out of the pub. Tom takes a breath,

'Well she's a whirlwind,' he laughs, his eyes crinkling at the corners in disbelief.

'I know she's my best friend in forever, we met at boarding school age eight and were pretty much inseparable the whole time until she went off to uni and I had to take over the yard. You ready to head out?'

I throw the now sticky cloth in the sink and round the bar to head out into the cool night. Tom skips in front of me, heaves open the door and we stroll out into the darkness, the cool night air filling my lungs with a sense of calm.

'I'm up here,' Tom points to an old pick up across the road.

I point to the Golf, 'Ok just follow me. Its only ten minutes up the road.'

I pull out of the car park and Tom follows along the winding Yorkshire roads, not a street light in sight. This is my homeland and I love it. I put my car in park and Tom pulls up beside me in front of the house.

'Follow me.' I lead him into the yard and around the corner to the trainer's house.

'Wait…' he puts his hand on my shoulder. I turn, 'I need to tell you something.' Panic rises in my belly. What on earth could he have to tell me? I hope he isn't a psychopath, I thought I was a good judge of character.

'I worked here a long time ago when I was sixteen, your dad accepted me as an apprentice.'

'Oh really, wow I must have been…' I try and work it out; I was never any good at maths.

'You were twelve,' he states.

'I must be honest,' I start embarrassed, 'I can't say I remember you very clearly, did you leave quickly or something?' He looks wary, a little stiff, he must have left quickly, my dad was very no-nonsense at times.

'What I'll say is that I was young, things didn't work out.'

'Well that's very mysterious,' I say amused. He is most definitely not amused so I continue, 'look, you were sixteen, I was twelve, it was a long time ago. As long as you didn't kill anyone I'm not that bothered. Did Ben give you a shitty nickname or something?' I chuckle, trying to lighten the mood; Ben was always giving the young apprentices awful names like Weak Will or Flappy Frankie, his eyes wander elsewhere, maybe remembering the time he was here last.

'Um, no he didn't and no I don't believe I did kill anyone,' he relaxes slightly.

'Come inside; I'd rather not have you freeze on your first night here.'

He follows me into the house and we are greeted by little Sam who spins around and yaps at our feet. Tom bends down to greet him, 'Hey there little guy,' he coos and gives Sam a scratch behind the ears.

'This is Sam the only real man in my life,' I laugh, Tom doesn't find it so funny he just gives me one of those intense, thoughtful looks again. I grab a key to one of the cottages and lead him across the yard to one where I know a room is made up. I place the key in the lock pulling the creaky plastic handle up as I do. The door creaks open and much to my relief the cottage isn't in complete disarray. He drops his bags and I turn to leave.

'I'll be up around half-six, see you in the morning.'

'Emma?'

'Yes?'

'Thank you.'

'Sleep well.'

Chapter Five

The next morning, I make my way into the yard to find Tom
is already mucking out the barn stables. He works quietly,
taking his time to talk to each horse, gently stroking each
one's nose while looking into their eyes. His dark hair flops
onto his forehead and a light sheen of sweat covers his
arms. He wears a grey sweat-shirt with sleeves rolled up to
his elbows, brown breeches ready for riding out and worn
trainers. Never did a man look so good in such simple attire.
It is obvious he is a natural horseman; my dad taught me that
you can tell a lot about a person in the way they treat a horse.
In Tom's case, I could tell he has a good heart and wouldn't
hurt anyone on purpose or am I being far too trusting of this
man who I'd invited into my home and my life?

'Morning Tom,' I chirp breezily.

'Morning,' he looks up from scooping a dropping into his
wheelbarrow and meets me with a bright smile as he wipes
his brow with his sleeve.

'You know you didn't have to muck them all out, I'm
perfectly capable of helping you.'

'I know, but I wanted to.'

'Ok, well seeing as you've finished, I'll show you the

mares, then I'll unlock the tack room and we can start riding.'

'Sounds like a plan.'

'Are you always this cheerful in the morning?'

'Not a morning person huh?' He smiles at me as we walk out of the yard and down to the fields at the back of the property where the mares spend their summers.

'Not until I've had coffee, put it that way.'

'You're just like my sister.' He chuckles.

'Really? What's she like?'

'Well, Phoebe is your age, twenty-one, completely horse-mad, just mad anyway.' He smiles, he was clearly very close to her.

'Does she look like you?' He meets my eyes when I ask this, and a small smirk breaks from his lips. Steady on, that was not an attempt at a compliment.

'Er I guess she does yes, she's a brunette about so high.' He gestures with his hand just above his shoulder. 'She was really excited that I was coming here.'

'Why?' I ask inquisitively. A small red tinge stains his cheeks. At this point, I clock on she thinks we're going to get together, and I can sense a blush creeps up my neck. This isn't good; I must have given him completely the wrong impression.

'Um, well she's seen your picture in the paper a few times,' he fumbles for words. We've reached the field gate and the mares begin to stride over.

'Look, Tom, I'm really glad you're here but right now I

just don't see myself with anyone. There's too much going on.'

'Wow she's nearly ready to foal,' he completely ignores me and enters the field to check out Iron Lady's large belly, running his hand gently along her dapple-grey stomach. Well, ok ignore that little titbit then. Once I've finished rambling on, he looks back to me. I now have eight pairs of eyes looking questioningly at me as Gaelic Blessing, Divine Intervention, Iron Lady and Tom have all gathered at the gate as I stand outside of the field basically talking to myself. Thanks guys!

'Um, yes, that's Iron Lady, who's in foal to Dark Angel, that's one of the reasons I asked you here as I've never foaled a mare before.' Cue Tom professing his expertise… not forthcoming… he continues to run an expert eye over the dapple grey mare. 'So, have you foaled a mare?' I say, hopefully.

'Yes, I have, a couple of times. In the next few days you should bring her in; it doesn't look like it will be long at all. I'll make her a straw box up later.'

'That would be great.' He's moved on to survey the other two mares' so I continue to introduce them. I feel a bit like a matchmaker. How ironic.

'The chestnut with the white star is Gaelic Blessing and the bay is Divine Intervention, she bred Divine Right the bay filly in the barn.' He nods in reply and we turn to make our way back up the yard.

'You take Silver Noble, I'll ride Divine Right.' I call out to Tom when we reach the barn. We tack up in silence and pull the two three-year-olds out while Flash kicks the door playfully.

'He's going to be a handful,' Tom calls back to me.

'He's going to win a big one, I just know it.' Tom turns and meets me with another soul-searing look.

'That so?'

'Mmhmm.' I nod emphatically.

'He's two years old, right?'

'Yep.'

'Well, we better get on with him soon.' I smile. My thoughts exactly. We ride up the gallops one behind the other. I quickly discover that Tom is very talented on a horse. At least I wouldn't have to call up Robbie to ride or for anything else! As we hack home, I ask Tom about his life as a jockey in America.

'So how many winners have you ridden?'

'Fifty in the states, ten over here.' Only ten winners on this side of the pond, a thought which creates a feeling of unease.

'So, you can't have ridden over here for very long?' I question further.

'No, not long,' is all he offers in reply. We ride on in silence for the remainder of the hack back to the yard. Tom takes Play Nicely out next while I cool off the others. When he rides back into the yard, he finds me talking to Flash.

'You're a naughty boy!' I laugh as he nips at my jacket zip. 'But don't worry, I love you anyway.'

'What's his breeding?' Tom asks to announce his presence back in the barn. I swat Flash away embarrassed to be talking nonsense to him. He is none the wiser and continues to nudge at my pockets for treats.

'He's by Galileo out of one of Daventhorpe's mares, my dad did a foal share.'

'Galileo huh?' Tom whistles under his breath.

I smile sheepishly. 'His near fore is so bent that Daventhorpe wanted him to be put down, but I persuaded dad to talk him into letting us have him. Daventhorpe doesn't have a clue, he thinks he's in a hole in the ground somewhere.' I stare into Flash's bright eyes, how any human could just put a horse down because they think it will be no good makes my blood boil. I saved him and now Flash is going to save me.

'Well, we better show him then.' Tom smiles as he looks, seemingly straight into my soul. *We.* Yes, we were going to do this. I barely knew Tom but something told me that he is either going to be the catalyst to my salvation or my biggest regret.

...

Later that afternoon we decide to start breaking in Flash. Tom goes to find the roller and lunge lines while I fetch a small bridle with a soft bit. He has had a bridle on before, but I had neglected to break him to saddle while concentrating on Daventhorpe's string. Flash looks perplexed that he is about to be put to work.

'You're going to become a racehorse mister.' I coo as I stroke his white blaze while Tom secures the roller.

'He listens to every word you say,' Tom speaks as he continues to fasten the buckles. I feel a rush of pride at his observation. 'I think he's good to go,' says Tom as he fastens the lunge line to the bit. I stand back as he leads him out of the stable and starts on his way to the arena. Once I shut the gate, Tom lets the lunge out and Flash immediately starts off in canter with his head in the air impersonating a gangly giraffe.

'Steady,' Tom calls as he pulls back on the rein. Flash takes his cue and breaks into a trot. 'Good boy.' After five minutes on each rein, we decide to call it a day.

I walk up to the pair of them and give Flash a rub on the forehead. 'Well that was less eventful then I thought it would be.' I chuckle.

'I should be riding him by the end of the week,' Tom explains.

Well, what a turn-up, I thought he was going to chill in that barn forever. 'We'll have to see how that leg holds up.' I eye his near fore warily, the vets had warned us that his joints might be weaker, but his forelegs had mostly self-corrected over the time we'd given him to grow. 'Are you ok to cool him off and feed the others? I need to go and see my dad in visiting hours.'

'Yes, absolutely.'

A few minutes later I'm making the all too familiar drive to the home. I enter the building to be greeted by Joyce as usual although today she isn't so chipper, which immediately sets me on red alert.

'Hi Joyce, is everything ok?'

'Yes dear, I'm fine. I believe Dr Lowther would like to see you briefly.' This does not sound good, my heart sinks.

'Oh ok,' I offer in reply. I make my way behind the reception and into a small study where I find an older man with wavy black hair and glasses sat behind an oak desk.

'Um, I'm Emma Williams. Is everything ok with my dad?'

'Please take a seat, Emma and I'll give you an update.' My legs feel weak, I have always known dad's prognosis isn't good and could never improve but I hoped it would be some time before I had to face this.

'Your father remains stable. However, his motor function continues to decline which is why you may find him in bed more often when you visit. Please don't be alarmed, this is expected, we will continue to monitor him closely.' He looks me straight in the eyes, but I don't feel reassured even though I know it is his intention.

'Ok, thank you. Please let me know if anything at all changes. Anything.' I repeat for emphasis.

'Yes, of course.' I leave the Doctors office feeling significantly more deflated. I climb the winding staircase and find my dad in bed asleep. He looks wizened and empty; it breaks my heart to see him like this. I tell myself that he is still here, still breathing and with me. I pull out a chair and sit beside him, taking his wrinkled hand in mine. He is clearly in a very deep sleep, he doesn't stir for the entirety of my visit but at least I have a little father-daughter time.

I make my way home to find Tom sat at the head of the table in the kitchen, my dad's chair, reading the Racing Post. He looks up at me when I enter but his smile drops when he sees my expression. 'What's wrong?' he jumps up and places his hands on my shoulders. God, he has such beautiful eyes. I momentarily pause my worrisome thoughts.

'It's dad, I'm worried about him.'

'How bad is it?'

'Well for starters you're in his chair and no one does that, and secondly, he didn't wake up the whole time I was with him.' Looking sheepish, he drops his hands from my shoulders.

'Sorry, my bad. Look sit down. I only came in to say that I've moved Iron Lady in from the field as she was starting to look restless.' I stay rooted to the spot in the doorway taken aback once again by his kindness. He pulls out a seat at the table and gestures for me to sit down. It takes a moment to register in my brain, but I gladly oblige and slump down into the seat with my elbows on the table, head in my hands. Tom rubs my back gently; once again, I feel on the verge of tears.

'Hey, don't cry.' How can a man I barely know already

know me so well? 'Chill out, eat some dinner and we can talk about it. A problem shared, right? Can I get you something to eat or anything?'

I look up at him, 'Thanks, there's some chicken salad I made a couple of days ago, enough for both of us.' He goes to the fridge and pulls out a large bowl.

'If there's anything I can do just let me know.' Tom replies as he fixes us both some food.

'Thank you but you've done so much already. God, I hate Daventhorpe, don't you just hate him?' I ramble.

'Err, he's definitely not my favourite person.'

'You know all of this is his fault. My poor dad. That man, that Daventhorpe, he's the reason I've lost everything, and he keeps taking things from me. Take, take, take, that's all he does.' Tom remains silent as I vent. 'Do you know how it went down? How he took my dad away from me?' Tom shakes his head silently.

'Sir, will you just trust me on this. The horses are not machines, we have to mind them and running them willy nilly is not going to help anyone.' My dad grates into the phone. I don't even need to ask who's on the other end its obviously Daventhorpe forcing my dad to do his bidding. 'I appreciate that York is the best track in Yorkshire but that's not going to make him run any better.'

A long pause ensues. 'Do not try to blackmail me. You and I both know that is not true.' My dad's voice breaks with anger and his face pales, he doesn't know I'm listening to this conversation. 'Goodbye Lord Daventhorpe I will see you at York next week.'

Dad paces around the kitchen, cursing under his breath, 'I wish I could tell that man to fuck off!' He angrily slaps the table, the door creeks in front of where I stand to eavesdrop. Dad spins around and sees me. 'Hello darl...' his knees appear to go weak, his face droops on one side and he falls onto the hard kitchen floor with a sickening thud.

'Dad! Oh my God!' I fumble for my phone to call an ambulance which arrives quickly thank goodness. The paramedics remain calm but I'm in shock, is this a bad dream? At the hospital, they diagnose a stroke, but the doctors gravely inform me that his condition will only worsen over time. I call my mum who couldn't give a shit, she tells me that, 'I'm sure he'll be fine Emma, he always is.' And promptly cuts off the line. And that's it, I'm alone.

'So that's how it happened, Daventhorpe's threats nearly killed him.'

Tom looks at me eyes wide and blows out a breath. 'That's... horrendous.' Is all he can offer. Not many people know how to react when I tell them although I've only told very few people as no one believes that Daventhorpe was trying to blackmail my dad. 'Do you know what he was threatening him with.'

'No. I guess, without a recording of that phone conversation, I'll never know but honestly, even if there was such a thing I couldn't face listening to it again.' By this time, Tom has finished eating, promptly pushing his chair back, breaking the silence as the legs grate on the floor. He places his plate in the sink, busying himself swilling it with water. He looks shaken by my story and I wonder why it's affected him so much. I make myself a promise as I swipe away the lone tear that has escaped down my cheek, I have to be strong now for dad. I will fulfil his legacy. I have to.

...

Later that night, I lie awake, staring at the dark ceiling, unable to sleep with all the thoughts whirling around in my head. *Why is my dad so sick? What was Daventhorpe threatening him with, and why is Tom so weird about the whole thing? How has he wound himself into my life so easily? I don't want to be a weak woman that needs a man to look after her.*

My phone rings. My first thought is dad, but when I pick it up and look at the screen, I see Tom's name flashing there.

'Hello?' I answer warily, 'What's wrong.'

'It's Iron Lady she's about to foal.' I jump out of bed and throw on a hoody over my pj's and hurry out into the yard. The warm light from the stable acts as a beacon and I rush towards them as fast as my legs will carry me. I pull open the door where I find Iron Lady laid on her side in a bed of straw with Tom standing quietly in the corner, letting nature take its course.

'Hi,' he says softly, 'I came to check on her and she was laid out ready to foal.'

I look on at the beautiful dapple-grey mare giving birth

right in front of my eyes. 'She's my favourite you know.' I look up at Tom, 'So beautiful and kind but noble and fiery at the same time.'

'Like you then.' My eyes widen and I blush at his compliment. I don't have anything in reply, so continue to watch in amazement as she pushes her back legs out and heaves her sides, trying to push her foal into the world.

Tom goes to her head, bending down to stroke her dark grey muzzle, 'There's a good girl,' he soothes. She fidgets some more trying to get comfortable, the straw rustling in response. Then something starts to move under her tail, two tiny hooves covered in white membrane peek their way out from under her jet-black tail.

'Tom, it's coming!' I say excitedly and we smile in unison. The foal's front legs emerge, with another push from the mother her foal slides further out. Then its nose pokes out, Tom quietly steps around and clears the fetal membrane from the foal's head and then with a rush the foal is born and lands in the straw. Iron Lady looks around at her new baby with wide eyes. I think it is the most precious moment I've ever witnessed in my life.

Tom gently shifts the foal around so that Iron Lady can lick her off. 'It's a filly.'

'She's gorgeous.' I breathe with a lump in my throat as we both watch the mother and baby share their first moments together.

We file out of the stable so mare and foal have time to

bond while we watch quietly over the stable door. 'I can't believe it, it's been such a long time coming.'

'She's a great mum.'

'She always has been. Her progeny always have her temperament, kind but take no shit.' I laugh.

'About what you said earlier…' Tom starts

'It's fine…' I cut him off, trying to avoid an awkward conversation embarrassed by my earlier ramblings.

'No, I want to tell you that…' he pauses and runs a hand through his brown hair, 'I'm really sorry that life has dealt you this blow, I know you don't deserve it and I just wanted to say that I hope I can be there for you and I wouldn't ever want to hurt you.' I stand there aghast at his words as he looks me dead in the eye meeting me head-on with no room for manoeuvre. 'You don't have to say anything; I just wanted you to know that.' My heart beats faster. I can't believe he just said all that. I hope he wouldn't ever hurt me. Heat wells inside me with an emotion I haven't felt in a long time, knowing that someone cares about me even a little bit, but something still niggles at me about Tom. He's been nothing but kind and decent to me, yet I still know very little about him and it bothers me.

We both turn back to watching Iron Lady and her baby interact. The little black filly tries to stand on her shaky legs, it takes her a few goes but after a while, she manages it and takes a greedy drink of milk from her mum who is back on her feet once again.

'What are you going to call her?' he questions.

I have a think for a minute and then it hits me, 'Legacy.'

'Legacy. I like it. You know she stood up quickly, she must be going to be a winner.' We both smile at the little filly who sucks hungrily at her mother for much-needed milk.

'Just like her mum.' We turn to look at each other our noses almost touching, we don't break eye contact as our breath mingles in the cool night air. Tom leans in a little closer his lips almost touching mine but still giving me the final say. I so desperately want our lips to touch but I break eye contact and pull myself back focusing once again on the mare and foal. The filly fumbles around in the straw on gangly legs oblivious to my inner turmoil. Tom stays in position. From the corner of my eye, I can see him squeeze his eyes shut and run a hand down his face. My heart is beating a mile a minute and I feel the urge to put distance between us. Not because I don't want to kiss him but because I do and that scares me more. I can't put my trust in someone when I know how easy it is for things to get messy but most of all, I'm scared.

'I… I'm sorry.' I stutter. Trying to avoid looking at Tom, I cast a glance back to Iron Lady and her beautiful baby. Tom must have been thinking the same because as I turn to go, he lets himself quietly back into the stable without a backwards glance.

Chapter Six

A week later and Tom is beside me as we pull up at the top of the gallops on Play Nicely and Silver Noble after working them both upsides. 'You know I think we could find her a race,' says Tom.

'I know! She flew up there.' I reply slightly out of breath from the back of Play Nicely. Both horses breathe heavily, and they snort clearing their airways from the exertion, the air fogs around them as the early morning mist surrounds us.

'When we get back, I'll have a look in the entry book. I think there's a race at York for her coming up.' I roll my eyes and laugh. Tom smiles across from me on Silver Noble 'Your favourite place, huh?'

'I love the course; I just don't like who I will see there.'

'Don't worry, I'll be there this time to punch him if we need to!' We laugh in unison, it feels good to have someone on my side for a change. Robbie never truly backed me, he just paid me lip service while he skulked around Daventhorpe.

'Are you happy to ride her?'

'Yes. If you want me to that is. It's fine if you want someone else.' His eyes fall to the ground as we walk on, the steady hoof beat of the horses and bird song our only company.

'I wouldn't want anyone else. I mean it.' I gaze at him, wishing him to stare into my eyes. He looks up still seeming unsure. 'If you're worried about Robbie…'

'No!' he almost shouts.

'Good because if he starts, it will be my turn to do the punching.' That comment seems to bring a smile to his face as we make our way back into the yard. I jump off patting the pretty bay filly on the neck. I love mornings like this when the horses go well and the sun shines. It makes you feel like anything is possible and no one could possibly sour your mood. All the thoughts of my parents, Daventhorpe and Robbie simply fall away.

I unbuckle the girth and pull off the saddle revealing white, frothy sweat. I lead my filly around to the hose, the cool water flushing it away easily.

After cooling off both horses, we make our way into the kitchen for breakfast. The Racing Post has been delivered and sits on the table. Daventhorpe's pudgy face graces the cover.

Lord D bullish as Dunkirk lines up for French Group 1 – Clive Jenkins

I recognise the authors' picture as the guy from the sales and shiver at the recollection.

'God he's a dick.' I seethe as I walk past the table to boil the kettle, 'Coffee?'

'Please.' Tom chuckles.

'You know that horse was off for six months last year with a suspensory and then he wonders why he isn't fit and doesn't win at York. Man's a muppet always has been, always will be. The sooner everyone sees that the better.'

'We'll show them.' Tom speaks from the table where he sits across from my dad's chair.

'Show them what?'

'What a lying, cheating bastard he is,' says Tom matter of factly.

I laugh without humour, 'Yeah? And how do you propose I do that?'

He looks me dead in the eye and says, 'Well you can start by training a winner next week at Ripon, there's a three-year-olds sprint handicap for Play Nicely.' It's then that I notice Tom sat in front of the entry book. I walk over and lean over his shoulder, he smells all manly, a mix of wood and sweat and horse.

I pull the book closer and note, 'That would suit her perfectly. You think she's fit enough?' I question as I look down at him to be met with a heated blue-eyed gaze.

'Well, there's only one way to find out.'

'You're right.' I say with conviction swiping the book off the table and promptly march into the office to make the entry. Tom chuckles and follows behind me. I click away on the BHA website selecting the race and adding Tom as the jockey. 'Tom Doyle, that name rings a bell.' I chuckle as I select him as the jockey. He stiffens slightly at my joke.

'What do you mean?' he breathes as he leans back and runs a hand through his hair.

'That is your name, right?'

'Oh, right yes, I thought you meant something else.' I click the submit button and breathe out a whoosh of air leaving my lungs. This is it, I'm making my come back on the racecourse. Daventhorpe is going to have kittens. *Shit.*

After breakfast, we decide that after a week's lunging and long-reining that the time has come for Flash to be ridden. We stand in the middle of the sand school, Flash is in full racing tack, Tom is all geared up, hat and body protector on, signature brown breeches and a black base-layer cover him. I hold Flash on the lunge line and Tom makes his way up the mounting block so that he can lean over his back and get him used to having weight there. I look up into his big round eyes and stroke his white blaze. 'Good boy, you've got this. You're a very good boy.'

'Ready?' Tom asks.

'When you are.' He leans gently over him; Flash's ears fly back and his head goes up unsure at the sensation on his back.

'Keep a strong hold on him.' Tom instructs 'He's thinking about this.'

I keep a strong and steady hand on the rein watching his eyes for any sign that he might freak. After a minute or two,

Tom stands back onto the mounting block and I give Flash a pat on the neck.

'Good boy, that wasn't so bad was it?'

'You're so soppy with him.' I stick my tongue out at that remark to which Tom gives a belly laugh.

'Ready to go again. If he's good, walk him around in a circle.' Tom prepares to lean over him again, Flash seems to know what's coming this time and shies away from the block, the whites of his eyes showing. I pull his head towards Tom so that he can't move his body out the way, he stands nicely once again and I give him a quick pat in reward. Tom leans over him and he fidgets slightly, 'Whoa big man.' Coos Tom. 'Ok walk him on a bit.' I do as he says and, walk him in a twenty-metre circle around the school. His eyes look back at Tom wondering what he is doing on his back but as he walks on, he settles. By the end of the session, Tom is riding him astride and Flash looks at ease.

'Two handsome boys together.' I sigh as I watch them walk quietly around the school. Tom chuckles from his position on Flash. I jump and bring my hand to my mouth, 'That was out loud, wasn't it?' Tom continues to laugh. Flash looks most put out that we aren't paying him enough attention and promptly leaps five feet in the air. Tom clamps his legs on and pulls at the reins which only makes him go faster. He breaks into a canter around the school, his back arched and rigid, unsure of what to make of Tom.

'Whoa, whoa.' Shouts Tom as he fights to bring him to a

stop, he circles him tightly, fighting to get a hold of him. The pair of them do the wall of death a few times while I stand frozen to the spot ready to peel one or both of them off the floor. Tom displays his mastery as a horseman as he finally brings the colt to a standstill in the middle of the school.

'Wow Emma, I think you've gotten yourself a good one here.' Tom laughs as I heave a huge sigh of relief that they both seem unharmed.

'I bloody well hope so!' I laugh as he gets off and comes to stand at his head. I lean down and run my hand down his near fore tendon checking for any heat or injury. Tom looks down at me with a furrowed brow as I make my evaluation.

'I think he's ok. Gosh, you both gave me a fright.' I breathe as I stand upright again.

'Come on Em.' he says as he flings an arm around my shoulders while he leads Flash back to the stables. I lean back into his strength, I'm worried that I like him too much but I'm too selfish to care right now as I revel in his warm touch.

...

I'm working my shift at the Winning Post later that day when a familiar mop of blonde hair enters the traditional Yorkshire pub. I could never miss him in a crowd, my body still seems in tune to him; however much my mind forbids it. My heart drops into my stomach; he's not alone. A gorgeous blonde girl with legs up to her armpits, a stunning figure, with striking green eyes, hangs on his arm and off every word he whispers into her ear. *Urgh,* I hate her already and then it hits me, I *do* hate her already because *she* is Daventhorpe's daughter Clarissa. I've only met her a handful of times, mainly at big race meetings. I remember her always being a bit ditsy and Daventhorpe would always tell her to go back to his private box when she would say something he didn't approve of. I think she was living in London while she worked in fashion but by the looks of it, she must have come back to live with him at Priory Castle.

They stand at the hostess stand to the restaurant where I am waitressing tonight awaiting service. Robbie is dressed in his signature button-down and slacks, his hair over-styled and parted down the middle. What did I ever see in him? Clarissa doesn't have a hair out of place her blonde locks ironed perfectly straight, her make-up flawless. She wears a short but not outrageous length skirt and a flowy dress top. They make quite the designer couple. Unfortunately for me, I am the only waitress in here tonight, so it looks like I'm going to have to face my darling ex and his new and improved girlfriend. Hooray for me! I make my way up to the hostess stand weaving my way around the other diners, trying to keep a low profile. As I get closer Robbie's head snaps towards me and he has to do a double-take, his jaw hitting the ground and making its way slowly back up again. Clarissa, however, obviously doesn't have the foggiest who I am as she continues to coo sweet nothings into his ear.

'Good evening, may I take a name.' I ask in my most

sugary sweet tone plastering on a fake smile.

'Er James' Robbie speaks almost unsure. I look down the list of booked tables and find his name. I can't believe I missed it earlier although I may have done a runner if I had known he was coming in.

'If you'll follow me please.' I instruct, pulling out two menus. I make extensive strides across the restaurant, hoping to get this encounter over with as soon as possible. I place them at a small corner table and take their drinks orders quickly, making my way back to the bar. I return and place a white wine for Clarissa and a pint for Robbie on the table as they peruse their menus.

'Are you ready to order?'

'I'll have the steak.' Robbie replies

'Do I know you from somewhere?' is Clarissa's reply

'Emma Williams.' I say blankly

'Oh yes, I know you. I totally know her.' She smiles, turning to Robbie, who sits with his hand on his forehead obviously stressed by the situation. 'How's the training going I love your yard it's super nice.' What planet is she on is my first thought, my second is she has no idea that her new beau is my ex. Sometimes ignorance *is* bliss.

'Babe, just place your order. She doesn't train anymore.' *Fuck you* is what I want to say but I remain silent trying to retain some dignity in this situation.

'Oh, sorry.' I'll give her credit she does look apologetic, quite a feat with a father like Daventhorpe. 'I'll have the

salmon. You have great hair though all ginger and frizzy.'
She smiles.

'Um, thank you, I think?' I stalk back to the kitchen to
put their orders in. I'll give her ginger and frizzy if she's not
careful, my hair is in a high ponytail tonight in some form
of control or so I thought, so I busy myself with other tables
trying to ignore the pair of them. I should feel hurt that he
has moved on so fast but honestly, I'm not at all surprised he
always made himself come first. I guess that's what makes
him a good jockey, but it still hurt that he didn't have the
decency to be upfront with me.

As I make my way to the kitchen to fetch their meals,
I see them sat across from each other, holding hands and
playing footsy under the table. I resist the urge to retch. Keep
moving Emma, keep on moving.

I quickly deposit their plates, avoiding all eye contact,
sprinting away from their table to take another table's order.
When I see they have finished eating I reluctantly make my
way over to their table to clear their dishes.

'I'm going to use the ladies room baby,' speaks Clarissa
as she gets up from her seat, patting down her skirt. I don't
make eye contact.

Once she has gone, Robbie grabs my wrist and starts,
'Emma…'

'What Robbie? What could you possibly have to say to
me?'

'It's not what you think?'

'You're dating Daventhorpe's daughter, ride for a ride huh? Nice. Classy.' I sneer, bringing my tray up to my chest, creating a barrier between us.

'Always *my* fault Emma, I'm not the bad guy you know, I'm just trying to get by in life you should do the same.'

'Are you joking me right now?' my voice rises an octave and the other diners shift in their seats uncomfortably. 'That's why I'm working in my old job waiting on wankers like you!' I promptly grab his pint off the table and pour it on his head. He doesn't know what to do sitting there soaked in sticky beer, his mouth wide open gasping for air. Clarissa promptly returns from the toilet and just stands with her mouth hanging open. Robbie stands bolt upright, slaps some money on the table, grabs her hand and hauls her out of the pub as fast as he can. I turn around when I hear a single person clapping behind me.

'That's my girl,' Clare gives me a wink and gets back to serving people at the bar. Normal service resumes after my little performance and everyone goes back to eating. Well, that felt good!

Chapter Seven

The day of the race at Ripon arrives. I feel sick, nervous, sweaty, and everything in between. I think Tom can feel my tension as he loads up the last of the kit into the lorry.

'It'll be fine, Emma." He says as he throws in the last bag while I jiggle around on my feet unable to keep still. I know Robbie will be there as Daventhorpe has a runner in the maiden stakes, but I am hoping to avoid both of them. Liv is going to meet us there as an extra pair of hands and moral support are going to be much needed.

'I'll go and get her.' I reply as I turn on my heel towards the barn to get Play Nicely who I find eating hay quietly at the back of her stable. 'Come on pretty girl; it's a big day for all of us today.' I already brushed her off this morning, so I quickly bandage her legs, put a fleece on her and walk her out of the barn and onto the waiting truck. Tom and I heave up the heavy ramp, and we're all set to go. We make the short journey to the racecourse in contemplative silence, when I say it's a big day for all of us, I'm not lying. It's my first runner in over a month since Daventhorpe took the horses, it's Play Nicely's first run of the season, and it's Tom's first ride back in England for five years.

I pull into the racecourse car park; it is a hive of activity with lorries and horses being unloaded for as far as the eye can see. Behind us, eager racegoers file into the racecourse, while owners and trainers fill up the adjacent car park in varying smart cars with blacked-out windows and shiny wheels. I hop out of the cab and Tom grabs the colours bag and his riding gear. He drops them to the floor at my feet which stops me in my tracks.

'Emma,' he starts, I look up into his eyes, a firm determined line set on his brow. 'I just wanted to say that you've got this and that no one can make you feel inferior unless you let them.' A rush of pride fills my chest and I place a hand over my heart.

'Thank you, good luck out there, be lucky.' He nods and heads off to the weighing room. I pull down the ramp and lead Play Nicely carefully down. She skits around, aware of her surroundings and the atmosphere of the racecourse. As I lead her into the stables, the stable staff from the other yards eye me warily. I keep my head down, concentrating on leading the filly safely into her stable. She sniffs around in her unfamiliar surroundings while my phone rings in my pocket and I pull it out to see Liv's name flash across the screen.

'Hi, are you here?' I answer

'Yes, I just wanted to warn you that DV is here with Ben and Robbie.' My heart drops. Even though I know they are going to be here, I hoped that maybe today they would all stay at home.

'Thanks, I'll see you in a bit, wait for me in the parade ring ok?'

'Ok, see you later.'

…

The first few races pass and Robbie wins on one of Daventhorpe's horses in the first race. Tom brings the tack to the stables and helps me saddle up. I never leave my horses alone at the races, so I have been awaiting his arrival for some time. My dad always taught me that you could never be too trusting; there are always people out there willing to play dirty. As he approaches, I take the time to appreciate him. He's dressed in white britches, black shiny race boots and a white vest top; he looks almost edible with his high cheekbones and floppy brown hair.

'All ok?' I ask as he hands me the saddle. He looks nervous, but I tell myself he's allowed to be so don't think much of it. He nods in reply and starts to place the number cloth on Play Nicely's back, number six. He then puts the weight cloth and saddle on. Luckily the saddle is of a decent size as although Tom is tall, he's light. When I helped dad to saddle up at the races he used to always curse at 'bloody Robert's rocking horse saddle' and we would both giggle.

She looks pristine, I've plaited her mane, put quarter marks on her bum and her coat gleams in the summer sun. Tom finishes pulling up the girth and turns to me while I hold the filly's head, he steps closer and I wonder what he's doing. My heart rate speeds up and I suck in a breath. All of a sudden, he places a light kiss on my right cheek and swiftly exits the stable. I stand there all flushed and red with a smile plastered all over my face. The filly biffs my chest as if to tell me that we've got work to do. I laugh lightly, gather my thoughts and open the stable door. Come at us every one!

I lead Play Nicely into the parade ring and see Liv standing in the middle with Tom who looks more serious than I've ever seen him before. Dressed in the navy and red of my dad's colours he looks quite the handsome man, gorgeous even. Those colours look like they belong to him, which makes me happier than ever. Robbie was a boy, but Tom is all man.

Racegoers lean over the railings deciding on the winner of the race. The racecourse is a buzz of activity. As I make my way around the ring, I spy Robbie getting his instructions from Charlie Davies, another local trainer. He doesn't seem to be listening as he bores a hole in the side of Tom's head with his eyes, a sneer planted on his lips. What a dick I think and carry on walking. I have almost made one full turn when I see him, Daventhorpe. He stands under the lone tree that covers the parade ring leaning against the bark, his dark eyes staring directly at me. He is wearing his usual tweed green suit and brown cap, his pudgy belly trying to break free. I try not to look him in the eye; his presence is enough to give me the creeps. Stay strong Emma, stay strong. After a few minutes, the bell is rung for the jockeys to mount. Liv and

Tom make their way over towards me. Liv takes the rein from me while I leg Tom on. I leg him up easily and he gives the filly a light pat on the neck while he gathers up the reins and puts his feet in the irons. Liv hands me back the lead rein which I unclip as I lead Tom onto the racecourse.

'Ok?' I ask as I begin to let them go.

'Yep!' and with that, it's out of my hands, Play Nicely breaks into a canter taking a strong hold down the course. It's all down to them now. The commentator announces the pair to the crowd as they pass the stands, 'Number six is Play Nicely ridden by Tom Doyle for Emma Williams, navy colours with red braces, owner Richard Williams.'

I make my way back into the parade ring to watch the race with Liv who looks a million dollars in a green pencil skirt and black dress top with her hair in a fishtail plait.

'You holding up ok?' she asks as I get to her.

I blow out a heavy breath, trying to calm myself. 'Getting there.' I smile. She steps closer to me and gives my shoulder a squeeze of solidarity. I can feel eyes on me, and I look across to see Daventhorpe still leaning against the tree with his arms folded. He nods as I look across at him. I snap my head back to the TV screen and will the ground to swallow him up.

'They're under starters orders.' The commentators' voice breaks out across the course. I blow out another breath. 'Come on filly.' I pray quietly.

The field breaks from the stalls and surges up the straight.

Tom eases Play Nicely to the front of the pack, her long easy stride eating up the ground. The rest of the field jostle behind her and Robbie, adorned in black and white colours, eyes Tom as his prey and moves in behind. They enter the final furlong and Robbie eases his ride up beside my filly. I grab onto Liv and we both shout them home, 'Go on Tom! Go on Tom!'

The field races to the line, Robbie strikes his mount with his stick which causes his horse to bump into Play Nicely who is pushed sideways for a stride. Tom pushes her on trying to correct her but it's too late and Robbie gets his horse's head in front on the line. I place my hands on my knees, happy with the run but deflated all the same. A second after nearly six months off is good going. Besides, she was only beaten by a head.

I make my way to the track to wait for Tom to pull her up and bring her in. Robbie gets in first and meets me with a smarmy smile. I resist the urge to give him the finger as I spy Tom riding up behind him. I give the filly a slappy pat on the neck, my hand becoming sticky with her sweat, before looking up to find Tom looking down seriously at me. 'Well done that was a good run.' I say with a smile

'I think she would have won if he hadn't bumped her.' He says fiercely. I lead them into the winner's enclosure where Tom dismounts. He doesn't say another word as he untacks and makes his way back into the weighing room to weigh in. Liv comes up behind me and gives me a consolatory pat on the back, 'Well done girl. What's up with him?'

'I think he thinks he should have won.' I shrug. We share a what are men like look and I proceed to cool and wash off the filly. I turn around to hear Liv speak, 'Look not now jockey person.' Robbie stands up to her and looks me in the eye pointing at me fiercely, 'We need to talk.' He shouts and stalks back into the weighing room. What is with everyone today?

'Horses away please. Weighed in. Weighed in.'

'I'll see you later; you need anything just call.' Says Liv as she gives me a quick side hug. I start to lead Play Nicely back to the stables giving her another slappy pat on the neck but as I make my way back through the parade ring, I find Lord Daventhorpe standing in my way in the middle of the exit. I look up to meet his dark, soulless eyes.

'You're playing with fire child,' is all he says as he turns to leave.

My last strand of decorum snaps, 'You can threaten my father all you want, but you are done threatening me.' I sneer.

His head snaps towards me as he hears the hidden meaning behind my sentence. He laughs soullessly, 'Careful what you wish for little girl, I've got things over your pretty little head that you can't even imagine.' With that, he stalks back into the crowd.

…

I settle Play Nicely back into her stable, careful to make sure she has stopped blowing, and run back across the course to meet Tom and get the colours bag. The racecourse has cleared out and only a few drunk and hard going racegoers remain. Unfortunately, I meet him and Robbie coming out of the weighing room simultaneously. Robbie spies me first and lunges towards me his kit bag flung to the floor forgotten.

'We need to talk.' He shouts as he stomps towards me, puffing out his chest.

'What Robbie?' I snap, 'I don't have time for this.'

'Don't you dare do this now.' Snaps Tom eyeing Robbie warily who chuckles to himself victoriously.

'Oh, dare me to do what pretty boy?' Tom's hackles rise and it looks like he is going to punch him.

'Would someone like to tell me what is going on?' I snap

'You have no idea who he is, do you?' laughs Robbie

'If your talking about him being an apprentice to my dad then yes I do have an idea.'

'Oh, Emmy, you've always been so naïve.'

'What are you talking about?'

'Remember when your poor old mummy left your shit show of a life? Well, guess who was in the middle of it all... little Tommy Doyle.'

'What? What do you mean?' I say turning to the pair of them. Robbie continues to laugh at my shocked expression while Tom's eyes drop to the ground, the colour draining from his face.

'Your mum didn't just leave because the winners stopped, she left because Tommy dearest here caught her at it in a stable with Daventhorpe.'

It takes me a moment to process; when it sinks in my legs go weak and all the air leaves my lungs. Tom comes into my line of vision and grabs both my biceps, 'It's not what you think.' He pleads.

I shrug free of his hold, he steps aside, and I look up to find Robbie still laughing to himself. I turn to Tom, 'Why… why didn't you tell me?'

'You like him, don't you.' shrieks Robbie, I remain silent, 'It gets worse!' he laughs. I stalk over to him, narrowing my eyes. He promptly stops laughing at my expression.

You.' I point at Robbie, 'put a sock in it and you,' I turn to an ashen-faced dejected-looking Tom, 'have a lot of explaining to do.' I turn on my heel, desperate to get away from both of them. I feel so hurt, betrayed and stupid that they both knew why my mum left and neither of them could tell me. I could have saved myself so much heartache over the years if only I'd been told the real reason why my mum left me. I'm not saying it would have hurt less, but maybe I wouldn't have blamed myself so much.

I keep running across the racecourse, the steady beat of my feet calming my racing heart and mind.

'Emma!' Tom shouts. I don't turn around even though I can hear him getting closer, 'Emma, wait!' Being a lot fitter and stronger than me, he eats up the ground and reaches me easily despite my best efforts to get away from him. He grabs hold of my right wrist in a vice-like grip, and I'm pulled around to face him. I don't meet his eyes, I simply look down at his hand, clasped tightly around my wrist. 'Please, Emma, let me explain.' I wrench free of his hold and take a step backwards wishing desperately to put some space between us, however much I hated him right now he still had such an effect on me.

'What Tom!' I snap.

'Please let me make this right.' He snaps back.

I run a frustrated hand down my face dropping it by my side, 'Oh God,' I yell at myself rather than Tom, 'he keeps taking people away from me. Everyone has pulled away from me because of him!'

Tom takes a step towards me, 'Then don't let him take anyone else, Emma, don't push me away. Let me explain; I didn't walk out of your life.'

'Yes, you did!' I scream back.

'No, I didn't... do you think I wanted to walk away from the best thing that's ever happened to me? Your dad, whatever anyone says about him, was the most loyal and decent man I have ever come across. He gave *me*, an unknown, inexperienced Irish boy a chance when no one else would. It wasn't my choice to walk away from that, Daventhorpe threatened me, wanted to pay me off, said he'd implicate me in some scandal. I left on my terms because I never wanted him to have anything over my head. Ever!' he replies fiercely.

'Did you tell my dad? Did he know?'

'Yes.' His eyes drop to the ground, ashamed, 'I went to him and told him. Maybe I shouldn't have, but I'm a decent man Emma, I didn't want anyone to get hurt, least of all you and for that I'm truly sorry.'

'Why… why didn't you just tell me? I let you in. I trusted you when I had no one.' I am aware of the sound of my voice rising again.

'Why are you yelling at me? I'm trying to make this right. I'm the only one here for you right now.'

At his admission, a lump gathers in my throat, 'Because…' I shout then lower my voice to a whisper, 'because… if you hadn't gone away then maybe I… I would have found you sooner.' My voice falters as I break eye contact with him. He steps towards me and places his palms gently on either side of my face, gently pulling me towards him but I can't bear to meet his eyes. I don't want to see the care and love I know I will find there. This isn't a man who would want to hurt me or anyone else. It wasn't his fault that he witnessed something no one should have to, and it wasn't his fault my mum was in that position. Ever since we met, he had only ever put me first and never shown me anything other than kindness but what bothered me the most was that whether I would ever be able to truly let him in knowing that maybe someday I would lose him.

'Hey… look at me.' he coaxes gently. I still can't, so he bends down slightly so that our noses nearly touch and our mouths align, 'Emma, look at me.' he breathes over my lips.

It takes Herculean effort to pull up my pupils to meet his. I was not wrong in my assumption, his beautiful blue eyes gaze right into my thoughts, my heart, my soul. 'I know it wasn't your fault. I just wish you'd told me.' I breathe as I cover his left hand with my own.

'I'm sorry.' He whispers before he gently places his lips over mine, for a moment I'm still unsure, but then I let myself feel again and I am putty in his hands. The kiss is tender, full of emotion and unspoken words of affection, care and apology. My hands find their way to his hard chest and he pulls me closer as he deepens our kiss. 'I'm sorry,' he breathes as he pulls away.

I place a hand on his heart and look up to meet his searing gaze, 'I know.'

Chapter Eight

'What happened?' asks Liv as she sits at the kitchen table the next day at breakfast. Sam sits proudly on her lap, like the king of the castle, as I stare blankly into my coffee mug, searching in its dark depths for answers.

'Nothing.' I say dumbly not meeting her narrowed eyes.

'Come on Em, I'm not stupid something happened, and I know you better than to accept that bullshit answer.'

I huff out a breath and allow a narrow smile to reach my lips. 'Tom was forced to leave because he found my mum and Daventhorpe at it in a stable.' I look up to find her wide-eyed stare directed right at me.

'You're joking.'

'I wish.' I laugh without humour.

'How did you find out?'

'Bloody Robbie came screaming at me out of the weighing room yesterday like a cockerel on speed.'

'And what did Tom say?'

'He said he didn't want Daventhorpe to have anything over his head and that he was sorry he kept it from me and then we...'

'And then you what?'

'We kissed.'

'You kissed!' Liv shrieks, Sam looks up at her with disgust. 'And why was that not the first thing you told me?'

'Because I'm confused.'

'About what Emma? I've seen the way he looks at you.'

'I'm scared Liv. If he kept this from me, what else has he got hidden? What if I let him in and then he just leaves or something happens to him or Daventhorpe threatens him or me or all of us?'

'Emma, stop, calm down. Leave everyone else out of this. This is between you and him. Don't make it more complicated than it needs to be. I know you're scared, but from the way you are right now he obviously is already a good way behind those walls so let him in, see what happens. You need to live your life Emma, you've always done the right thing, taken the safe option, let go, see what happens, I'm sure he'll be there to catch you.'

'Catch me?'

'When you f...'

Just then Tom comes in from the yard after cooling off Divine Right from her exercise. Sam hops off Liv's lap and spins circles around him, wagging his tail playfully. Tom bends down to greet him and gives him a scratch behind the ears.

'Since when does he like you more than me?' jokes Liv completely oblivious to the effect her words have had on me, so I give myself something to do by making my way over to the coffee pot.

'Morning Liv.' Replies Tom with a chuckle as he comes to join me at the coffee pot, he leans in close our bodies aligning as we both fix ourselves a hot drink. When I turn around, Liv gives me a scheming look which I try to ignore as we both sit opposite her at the table. As he sits down, Tom flops an arm over the back of my chair. I sit a little stiffly trying not to lean back to feel his touch, however much I want to. I can tell Tom is gazing at me, confused.

'I'm going to tack up the naughty child' says Tom lifting from his seat referring to Flash who was beginning to show us we needed to up his work.

'Ok, I'll follow you out.' We stand in unison and deposit our mugs in the dishwasher. Before I can leave, Liv stops me and pulls me into a hug, 'Don't overthink it Em, just be, ok? Breathe, live, love.'

'I know. Thanks Liv, I mean it. What would I do without you?' I pull out of her embrace.

'Now go and see to lover boy and that crazy horse before you go all mushy on me.' she laughs.

I make my way into the yard to find Tom holding Silver Noble for me, all ready to go. His eyes light up as I approach him. 'Thank you very much for tacking up my horse.' I chuckle as he moves behind me to leg me on.

He throws me up with ease using only one hand, 'You sure you're not the jockey in this relationship?' he laughs as he gazes up at me, 'You don't weigh a thing.'

'Nah, leave all that to the professionals.' I say, a little caught off guard at his use of the word relationship. Is that what we are in now? A relationship?

'Professionals huh? Not sure you could call any of us that!'

'Who said I was talking about you?' I mock.

Tom brings a hand to his heart and grimaces, 'You burn me woman, burn me.' he jokes as he retreats into the barn to fetch Flash who appears snorting with his tail in the air, jig jogging next to Tom who leads him with two hands trying to keep a hold of him. 'I think we need a professional for this one Em.'

'Nah, you'll do.' I laugh as Liv makes her way into the yard right on cue to leg Tom onto a very fresh Flashdance. She grabs one of the reins and circles him around her while using the other hand to lift Tom onto the colt.

'Bye, guys. You,' she points at me, 'Ring me ok?' and waves as she makes her way to her car.

'Let's see what you've got Flashy boy.' I smile down at my pride and joy as we walk out of the yard in unison toward the gallops. 'Follow me down the woodside and then as we turn into the straight, come up on Silver's quarters and see if he'll take you upsides me.

Tom nods in recognition all joking forgotten as he shortens his reins, getting ready to ride Flash through his first real test as a racehorse.

As soon as the horses' feet hit the woodchip, they

instinctively start to jog and get ready to gallop. Even though Flash has only been cantering up steady for the last few weeks, he has a racehorse's intuition and spirit to go fast and be the best. I push my body weight forward and Silver breaks into a canter, by the sound of Flash's footfall behind me I hear Tom do the same.

We take it steady to the bottom of the gallop and make the long turn towards the top, gradually building up the pace. As we make our way into the straight, I can hear Tom and Flash behind me getting closer. The air rushes around us and I instinctively lower my body becoming more streamlined. From the corner of my eye, I see Flash's white blaze coming up beside me. Then he moves up faster in line with Silver and he starts to move slightly in front while remaining upsides. In shock, I urge on Silver a little more to keep pace with the boys, but Flash remains at ease and floats across the woodchip until we reach the top and pull up. I turn to Tom a little stunned at Flash's performance, 'Well shit.' I shout out of breath.

'Wow, Emma, I think you've got yourself a superstar.'

'Yes!' I shout, looking up to the sky. 'I knew it Tom! I just knew it!' Flash flicks his head and swishes his mane, wondering what all the commotion is about.

Tom reaches down and pats Flash fondly. 'Honestly, Em that's the best feeling a horse has given me in a long time.'

My face can't contain my smile as we walk home in the morning sun. 'Do think we should enter him?' I ask, turning to Tom.

'No harm in having a look at what races there are.'

A sudden ball of nerves fills my stomach at the prospect of revealing him to the world but most importantly revealing him to Daventhorpe. 'Daventhorpe will go crazy.' I reply, a slight tremble to my voice, 'Maybe I should just keep him at home.'

'Em,' Tom says frustrated, 'We can't live our whole lives afraid of what one man might do, think or say. This horse is way too good to sit in a stable all his life. He could be your salvation Emma. The start of something more and besides he's in your dad's name so what's Daventhorpe going to do about it. He can't.'

'You're right. Let's do this thing.'

When we get back to the yard, I cool off Silver Noble then make my way into the office. There is a race for two-year-olds over seven furlongs a week from now at Thirsk. The perfect starter race for Flash. I stare at the writing on the screen, hovering over the submission button on the mouse, a sick feeling settling in the pit of my guts. I have a horrible feeling this is going to cause a lot of drama.

Tom pulls open the door and makes his way toward me. 'Well?' he places his hands on my shoulders from behind standing while I almost slump in the computer chair. 'There's a race at Thirsk next week over seven furlongs.'

'Have you entered it?' he prompts.

'Emma?' I sigh and turn to face him.

'Well, not technically, I need to press submit.' I blush and look down at my hands

'Do it Em. Believe in us.'

…

'Pint.' States the same slimy guy from my first shift. I swallow my frustration at his rudeness and set about pulling his pint. I place it lightly on the bar while he throws some change across the sticky timber surface.

'Might be comin' to see you darlin', been making some enemies lately.' He slurs

'Excuse me?' What was with this weirdo, 'What's your problem?'

'I ain't the one with the problem darlin'.' He snarls as he saunters off with his pint, leaving me a little rattled and shaken. Clare comes up to stand beside me shaking her head in disapproval.

'Who *is* that?' I question.

'Smithy Butler, ex-jockey of Daventhorpe's from many years ago. No one really knows what he does these days just turns up at the pub now and then.'

Daventhorpe. Shit. He must know. He already knows, I panic. 'I don't remember him. He mustn't have lasted very long, or I was very young. Dad never mentioned him.'

'Knowing Daventhorpe, there was probably a scandal.' Shrugs Clare, who returns to the kitchen, leaving me to my inner turmoil. Typical Daventhorpe using and abusing everyone and everything for personal gain. Worrying about

Daventhorpe's never-ending agenda sours my mood for the rest of the evening, my nerves are shot and by nine o'clock, I am extremely ready to go home.

'Knock knock.' A familiar voice taps on the bar. I swing around to find Tom leaning over the countertop, his hair wet from a shower, dressed in a white t-shirt and black jeans, a crooked smile on his face. At the sight of him, I immediately feel happier. I lean over and give him a quick hug across the bar top. After my talk with Liv, I feel lighter and happier to let things happen.

'Miss me much?' he chuckles

'It's been a long night.' I sigh, 'Can I get you anything?'

'Well, would it be cheesy to say I mainly came to see you, but I could definitely use something to eat.'

Right on cue, Clare returns from the kitchen, 'Did someone say eat? Sounds good to me. Emma dear you knock off for the night and order something for yourself and Tom on the house of course.'

'Thank you.' I smile and hug her.

Tom orders scampi, I order salmon. We take a seat at an empty table in the restaurant. I decide to break the silence first, 'Look, Tom, about what happened at Ripon, I'm sorry I keep pushing you away I'm just…'

'Scared.' He finishes for me as he reaches for my hand across the table, 'I know and I know I shouldn't have kept my secret but when I started to get to know you, I couldn't bear the thought of what it would do to you if I just came out with it.' He squeezes my hand a little tighter.

'Looking at it from your point of view I understand, but I want you to promise that you won't keep anything like that from me ever again.'

'I promise Emma. I would never hurt you intentionally.' He meets me with a gaze of sincerity.

'You know I still can't believe how well he worked this morning.' I say, changing the subject, 'Although I think Daventhorpe already knows.' Tom's head snaps up as he pulls his hand from mine.

'What do you mean?'

'Do you remember Smithy Butler?'

'Name rings a bell but no, not really. Why?'

'He was in here earlier, and he said that he might be coming to see me because I was making enemies. It scared me a bit. I'm not going to lie.'

Tom visibly tenses and his jaw sets in a hard line. 'I won't let anyone hurt you Em. I promise you that.'

A rush of warmth wraps around my heart and tears spring to the backs of my eyes. I reach across the table to take his hand and give it a quick squeeze; his gaze unwavering.

'You don't think it would come to that, do you?' I shiver with a surge of dread filling my veins.

'I wouldn't let it.' he states unquestioningly.

I smile at his protectiveness. It feels so good to have someone who wanted me for me. Our food arrives and we eat in contemplative silence.

'What do your family think to you riding again in England?'

'They're all thrilled.' He smiles, 'I think they missed me while I was in the US, especially my sister.'

'Phoebe, right?'

'Yeah, I think she's going to come over and visit in the autumn. She's desperate to meet you.'

'Well, any of your family is welcome.'

After our meal, I wave goodbye to Clare and we make our way out into the cool night air. Tom settles into his stride beside me; a protective arm flung around my shoulders as I lean into him. As we make our way down the steps of the pub, a force bashes into me from the side and the wind is driven from my lungs. I gasp for air, the sour smell of alcohol filling my nostrils. I fling my arm out, ready to break my fall. Luckily, I don't have to as Tom's strong arms wrap around my waist, pulling me into his chest and I hang onto him for dear life.

'Should watch what you're doing.' An all too familiar voice slurs. I whip my head around, pulling out of Tom's embrace, to find Smithy wildly staring at me. I open my mouth to say something, but I don't have to.

'I don't have a fuckin clue who you are or what your agenda is, but you stay the hell away from this girl or you will have me to deal with.' Tom swears angrily. I step back, unsure of what is about to go down. Tom, in tune to my movement, reaches out for me and pulls me into his side with his arm around my waist. I resist the urge to cry as Smithy looks me up and down, his stare settling on my chest. Tom notices, his jaw visibly ticking, and he pushes me behind him, shielding me from this disgusting man. Smithy smiles smarmily and laughs in Tom's face.

'Don't say I didn't warn you.' he slurs before hobbling off into the night.

When Tom is sure he is gone, he turns to face me; a lone tear escapes down my cheek and I will it away. Tom gently wipes it away with his thumb and envelops me in a hug, his hand holding the back of my head. I inhale his scent, trying to calm my racing heart and shot nerves, squeezing my eyes shut as I grip his strong shoulders for support.

'Come back with me. We can pick up the Golf in the morning.' I have no possible objection so follow him over to his truck. He opens the door for me, and I expect him to go around and get in the driver's side; instead, he leans down and buckles me in making sure I'm safe. It seems more for his own peace of mind than for my own. Before he starts the engine, he takes my hand and places a light kiss on my palm. 'I keep my promises, Emma. Always.'

Chapter Nine

'I'm going to pick up the feed order.' Tom informs me as we sit at the kitchen table the next morning after a busy start to the day exercising the horses. Sam sits on my lap, and I cuddle him close, resting my head on his.

'Ok, Sam and I are going to check on Iron Lady, aren't we?'

We make our way out of the house towards the fields, but I stop in my tracks when an infamous black Audi floats into the yard.

'What now?' I groan as I make my way over to Robbie's fancy car. He struts around to me, wearing the usual button-down and brown loafers with no socks, dirty blonde hair perfectly gelled into place.

'Emma.' He states as he comes to stand in front of me, running a polished hand through his blonde locks.

'What do you want?' I snap, unable to hide my annoyance at his presence here, especially after the stunt he pulled at the races.

'I think we both know why I'm here. Don't you?'

Dread fills my stomach, but I decide to play him at his own game. 'Enlighten me.' I state in a bid to sound bored.

'Come off it, Emma, you know Daventhorpe hit the roof when he saw you kept that colt, he told your dad to put it down.'

'Well, he has no right; he has no claim to him whatsoever all the paperwork is in dad's name.'

'Don't run him Emma, who knows what he'll do if he wins.'

'Well, let's hope he doesn't.' I retort a little shook.

'God, Em be serious! I'm just trying to help you out here.'

My resolve snaps and anger boils within me, 'How dare you even show your face here Robert, you don't give a shit what happens to me. You've made that perfectly clear.'

'You always blame me; I've told you before I'm just trying to help you out.' He bellows, his arms waving in all directions for effect.

'Fine then, did you ever love me?' I question pointedly.

'What kind of question is that?' he asks as his face pales

'So that's a no then.'

'Don't put answers in my mouth.' He shouts

'Well don't come here to do Daventhorpe's dirty work that he's too cowardly to do himself.' I scream back. He takes a breath steadying himself.

'I may not be the man you always dreamed of Emma, but that doesn't mean I don't care.' He replies measured, 'You say I never cared for you or paid you any attention, but I remember how much you loved that horse, so keep him here and be happy that he is.'

'Are you finished?'

He flings his arms up in surrender and turns on his heel, 'You know where the gate is.' He revs the engine for effect, winding the window down as he pulls out.

'Don't say I didn't warn you.' he points accusingly at me. As he pushes the accelerator, dust flies up, and he narrowly misses Sam in his attempt to make a dramatic exit.

'Mind the dog, you Neanderthal.' I shout at the car's retreating form and rush over to gather Sam into my arms. I squish my face into his fur, inhaling his doggy smell. My heart is racing once again, what is wrong with everyone threatening me left, right and centre. I plop Sam back onto the ground, and he scurries after me as I make across the yard to the American barn. At the sound of my footsteps, Flash pops his head out over his door. I stand in front of him and look at his majestic head filled with his white blaze. I look into his eyes and scratch his forehead a little,

'What are we going to do Flashy?' I ask more to myself than to him, but instead, he answers me with a biff in the stomach. 'Ow.' I groan and then laugh. His insolence stirring up some determination within me. I hated all the threats that were flying around me, but I would not bow under pressure; if I did, I'd be avoiding everyone and everything all my life.

My phone starts to buzz in my pocket, and I pull it out to see the care home's name flash across the screen and all manner of thoughts cross my mind.

'Hello?' I ask, my voice shaking a little.

'Hello, is that Emma? It's Dr Lowther. Your father is extremely stressed. I think his brother upset him and we cannot calm him down.'

'His brother?' I question, 'He doesn't have a brother.'

That rattles the doctor and he starts to stutter, 'Oh, um, right, I see. I think it's best if you come in and see if you can calm him down.'

I start to run for my car, Sam scampering at my heels. I turn the corner and, 'Shit!' I scream at the absence of my car. I hadn't been to pick it up since last night. I scramble for my phone to call Tom. He picks up after a few rings, 'Tom, where are you? I need to get to the home.' I screech my voice cracking with the onset of tears.

'Whoa, Emma, what's wrong?'

'Where are you?' I ask again, 'I need you to get me to the home.'

'I'm about five minutes away. I'm on my way.' I click off the call and wait for him at the gate, pacing up and down. I am a tornado of emotions and unanswered questions. Daventhorpe must have got to him. Tears threaten again. This is all my fault; I've created all this myself. As I pace, Sam follows my every step and I smile down at him.

'Come here, you silly thing.' I coo and motion for him to jump into my arms, and he duly obliges. I scrunch my face into his fur. After a few moments, Tom tears up the drive dust flying up around his tyres. I heave open the passenger door with my free hand and throw Sam into the truck before me. Tom's eyes are wild as he watches me climb in, 'What's happened?' he asks as he puts the truck in drive once again.

'The doctor rang and said that dad's brother went to see him, and he upset him, but he doesn't have a brother. Daventhorpe must have got to him. That's the only thing that makes sense. I'm the only family he has here.' I rattle off.

'Shit.' Shouts out Tom as he grips the steering wheel a little tighter, his knuckles turning white. The passing scenery blurs outside the truck windows as we speed down the narrow lanes. Panic rises inside me, my breathing becoming shallow. 'Breath Em, you won't be able to calm him down if you're panicking yourself.' Tom reaches across, finding the back of my neck, steadily rubbing it with his thumb.

We finally pull up the drive of the home and before Tom can put the truck in park, I yank open the door and race for the entrance. I am greeted by a huddle of worried voices talking in hushed tones. They recognise me instantly and immediately break out of their hurried discussions. Tom jogs in behind me, anxiety marring his beautiful features.

'Miss Williams,' the doctor moves forward to greet me, 'firstly, may I apologise for the circumstances for your visit.' I glance at him in disbelief, how can he be so calm when my father's rights have been so clearly violated.

'I hate to be rude doctor, but I'm going to see my dad and we can discuss this later.' He looks a little taken aback but motions me on nonetheless.

'I'll wait here for you.' Tom calls after me as I make my

way up the stairs toward my father's room, the doctor hot on my heels.

'I can take it from here doctor,' I announce eager to reach my dad.

As I open the door to his room, a nurse sits by his bed, rubbing his arm trying to soothe him, she stands abruptly as I move over to take her place. My dad's eyes are wide with fear and his breathing shallow. I grab his hand as I lower myself to sit on the edge of his bed, 'It's ok daddy, I'm here now.' I whisper. He instantly calms and brings our joined hands to his lips and places a tender kiss on my thumb. The gentle action has me imploding on the inside, the contrast in our hands is stark and profound, his wizened grey, veined hand wrapped around my youthful, healthy palm. He looks up at me, his sunken, once green eyes search my own; my heart breaks in my chest. 'I love you so much.' I breathe into his thin grey hair, gently placing a tender kiss on top of his head. He smiles up at me and squeezes my hand a little tighter. I decide to try and brace the subject of my impromptu visit, 'Was it him daddy? Was it Daventhorpe?' He instantly tenses and I regret my decision to ask him, but I needed to know what we were dealing with, and by the looks of the staff around here, incompetency is rampant.

'Shh, it's ok.' I soothe, 'He can't hurt you anymore. I won't let him.' I sit with him a little while longer, just being in his company, comforting him in any way I can. A small knock on the door announces the doctor's arrival in the room.

'May I speak with you,' he asks nervously, looking from me to my dad and back again, 'in private.' I give my dad one final kiss and make my way out of his room. I glance back quickly to find him smiling gently at me. I smile back and raise my hand in a small wave. I make my way with the doctor to the reception to find Tom pacing up and down, his face skewed into all kinds of anger and frustration.

On seeing my presence, he surges towards me, 'How is he? Was it him? Can I do anything?'

'Shall we go into my office so we can discuss this?' answers the doctor. I gesture for Tom to follow and he falls into step behind us.

'Firstly, I can only apologise for what has happened today. It was a complete misjudgement on our part. I completely understand if you wish to take any action you deem necessary.'

'I'm sorry, what?' I asked completely aghast at his bluntness. I can feel Tom getting riled up beside me, but I choose to ignore him and continue to listen to the doctor.

'Well, I take full responsibility for not looking further into the gentleman's story when he arrived this morning.'

'What did he look like?' I ask clipped

'Well, er, he was wearing a brown fedora.' Daventhorpe's most well-known accessory.

'Is this a joke?' laughs Tom sadistically behind me. I turn to set him with a stare to shut up, I don't want to make this any more of a scene than it already is.

'Sorry you are?' the doctor asks.

'Emma's boyfriend.' He replies matter of factly. My mouth drops open as I watch their heated exchange.

'Oh, Robert, hello.'

I snigger, could this day get any crazier. How does he know what my ex-boyfriend is called and not the well-known fact that my dad is an only child?

'Er no. Are you that incompetent, honestly,' replies Tom blowing out a frustrated breath and turning in a circle running a resigned hand down his face and dropping it loosely again at his side. The doctor shifts uncomfortably from foot to foot.

'Right.' I speak up, trying to take back control of this situation and make up for Tom's apparent rudeness. They have taken good care of my dad for a long time, and I don't want that to stop now. 'I appreciate you holding your hands in the air, but in future, I would ask you that my dad has no visitors of any kind unless I am here. Plus, the man that came to see him is the honourable Lord Daventhorpe who has a vendetta against all of us, so if he so much as drives past the gates of this place, I want to know. Ok?' I meet the Dr with a harsh stare to get my point across.

'I understand Miss Williams. You have my most sincere apologies.'

'Thank you, doctor, we have to go, but please call me if there's anything at all.' I turn on my heel and grab Tom's hand to pull him out of the room before he punches the doctor square in the face.

'What was all that about?' I pull him around to face me as we reach his truck. Sam jumps up at the driver's window, yapping for attention.

'He is completely incompetent Emma. Oh, sincere apologies, my ass. It should never have happened in the first place. Who knows what the hell could have happened?'

'You think I don't know that Tom?'

'Well, it didn't look like that in there.'

'You didn't have to be rude to him!' I screech, 'and oh, "I'm her boyfriend", when did you decide that?'

'Seriously, Emma?' Our stares meet head-on everything around us falling into insignificance. 'I promised to protect you, and I keep my promises.'

'I get that, but he's my dad. I'll take care of the situation.'

'Emma, for goodness sake, don't you get it. Your situations *are* my situations now!'

I've been on my own for so long, forced into the independence I never wanted that I have erected a sturdy wall around myself. I've made it that I don't have to depend on anyone to avoid the inevitable heartbreak of losing them, but Tom seems different. He has already shown an understanding of me that I don't even know myself. I realise at this moment that I need to let him in, let someone else take care of me rather than taking care of everyone else. Not as a weak woman that needed a man to save the day but as an equal.

'I know.' I whisper, breaking free from my thoughts, 'I'm

sorry.' He strides toward me, places his hands on my upper arms and looks down into my eyes.

'I'm sorry too. I know I gave him a hard time but you're my family now, that means your dad too, and when he thought I was that shit head Robbie well, that just pissed me off.'

A wide smile breaks free across my face and I begin to laugh, 'That was pretty funny.'

Tom returns my smile, joining me giggling as we smile straight back at each other with no walls between us. He pulls me into a tender embrace.

'Let's go home.' He smiles as he grazes my temple with a light kiss.

We both buckle into the truck and Sam immediately jumps on my knee.

'Do you want to pick up your car on the way back?' Asks Tom reading my thoughts.

The journey home is a lot lighter than the one earlier but, brick by brick, the worries start to fall back on me.

'Robbie stopped by earlier?' I begin hesitantly, unsure of what Tom's reaction will be.

'And…' he prompts

'He told me not to run and keep him safe at home with me because he knows how much I love Flash.'

'Love? He wouldn't know the first thing about that.' Spits Tom. I look across at him in disbelief.

'Um.'

'Well,' he continues, 'he let you go.' A warm swell of a feeling I can't describe fills my chest, so I simply turn and smile appreciatively at him.

'It's true.' He says nonchalantly as he shrugs his shoulders.

'You're something else, Mr Doyle, something else.'

Chapter Ten

A week later and Flashdance is about to run his first race.

Thirsk racecourse is covered by overcast skies and a light but unrelenting rain that soaks any hardy racegoer keen enough to journey out to the races in the middle of the week. I make my way up the steps to the weighing room, eager to get out of the worst of the weather. Tom leans over the barrier that divides the scales from the rest of the area, the saddle, cradled in his arms, a look of deep contemplation settled on his face. As I approach, he steps from the rail and passes the saddle across to me. We don't say a word. We both know what is depending on this lowly six-runner seven-furlong novice stakes. The usual hustle and bustle of the weighing room is unapparent. Jockeys and trainers are sparse. This trend continues as I make my way back across the course toward the stables. The racecourse is eerily quiet and not just because of the weather. A sense of foreboding puts me on edge as I scan the horizon for any signs of Daventhorpe, Robbie, or any of his other cronies. I feel like a prey animal being stalked by a pack of lions aware that trouble is brewing but unable to pinpoint the direction of the attack. I pick up the pace and lengthen my stride toward the stables where

Liv guards Flash against any unwanted visitors.

Liv is seated on an upturned bucket while reading the race card and tutting to herself while Flash watches on quietly. I give Flash a quick rub on the forehead, he looks all grown up with his mane plaited.

'What's got you all wound up?' I snicker.

'Well,' she starts dramatically, 'apparently, you've got no record with first time out two-year-olds.'

'Don't take it personally,' I chuckle, 'my record is crap because Daventhorpe always made me run them way before they were ready. What else does it say?'

'Well, he's the favourite. I suppose that's not surprising with him being by Galileo.'

'And his mother is a half-sister to Priory Castle so you could say he's a sure-fire winner.' I laugh and slap my forehead. 'There's no such thing as a sure-fire winner with horses. They literally have no idea what he's been through.'

We make our way into the stable and set about putting on the tack. First, I place the weight cloth, then the pad and finally the number two cloth. I fasten the small red leather saddle with a thin elastic girth and secure it with a matching surcingle. Flash is so calm the entire time; it is like he has done it all before when, in reality, any normal two-year-old would be fretting at their unfamiliar surroundings.

I go to take the lead rein from Liv but she stops me, 'I'll lead him up Em. You're the trainer, you need to be with Tom.'

'Ok, you said it. If he gets difficult, I can take him off you.'

'You worry too much.' She rolls her eyes

'Wagons roll then.' I wave them on as I give Flash a pat on the neck.

We are the last runner to reach the parade ring, but secretly, that was my plan as I wanted to draw as little attention as possible to us and, most importantly, time to keep Flash relaxed.

The jockeys approach and I waste no time in getting Tom on board and the pair of them down to the start. 'Are you happy with what you're doing?' I ask Tom as we approach Flash, who is quietly following the other two-year-olds around the paddock. He nods in reply completely focused, I don't need to give him instructions, he has a race plan in his head, and I trust him completely.

Liv unties the lead rein from the bit and lets Tom and Flash go to canter down to the start. A rush of emotion fills my chest and tears well at the back of my eyes. I never thought I'd ever see the moment he set foot on a racecourse. Dad would be so happy and proud to see the little gangly colt foal he kept the faith in fulfilling his destiny.

I make my way along the course weaving through the other racegoers toward the big screen to watch the race. Liv comes to join me, kneading the lead rein between her hands, her knuckles turning white.

'Gosh, I'm so nervous, and he's not even my horse.' she

tells me as she jiggles around on the spot and wipes her forehead, which was damp from the rain, with her jacket sleeve.

'It's funny, isn't it?'

'What?'

'How quickly the love grows and how much you want it.'

'I've never wanted anything more than this right now.' She laughs, 'And I've got a law degree.'

I turn my attention back to the runners who are beginning to be loaded by the stall handlers. Butterflies whirl in my belly as we get closer to race time. I blow out a huff of air, trying to quiet my racing heart. I wince momentarily as Flash pauses on entry to his allocated stall of three, puts his head up and looks back in fright. We practised stall starts plenty of times with him at home, but until they are faced with the prospect of them at an unfamiliar racecourse, you never really know if they will go in and, most importantly, come out with the rest of the runners. Tom shows his horsemanship as he gives Flash a quick pat and urges him forward with a squeeze of his legs. Flash obliges, taking the last few steps forward into his stall. Relief washes over me, but this is only academic as the race has yet to start.

'Last to go in is Black Barton and Shane Wilson.' Announces the commentator. A momentary pause ensues as the final handler emerges from the stall and ducks under the rails in the middle of the course.

'And they're off… Flashdance breaks smartly and shows early pace leading the field into the bend. Black Barton in the green jacket tracks him in second with Euro Flyer upsides in third and London Lover tracks them midfield. The blue colours of Hester is behind these pushed along and Crystal Letters struggles to go with them after missing the break and trails by six lengths.'

I am thankful for the big screen as the field make their way down the back straight as the low-lying cloud makes viewing from the stands difficult. Flash's easy stride eats up the ground making the other runners appear laboured. Tom sits unmoving and guides him easily into the bend, ready to take on the home straight.

'Flashdance and Tom Doyle set the pace as they enter the home straight with Black Barton shaken up by his jockey in behind. London Lover makes headway as he hits the rising ground up the straight with Euro Flyer lying in fourth. Hester and Crystal Letters trail the leading quartet and look one-paced at best entering the final two furlongs. But it's Flashdance that holds the lead as they enter the final furlong and he's stopping for no one. Black Barton and London Lover give chase, but this is some performance. Tom Doyle has not moved on this first time out juvenile and he goes on to score readily by seven no eight lengths. You've witnessed something here today ladies and gentlemen. One for your notebooks I'll say. London Lover stays on for second with Black Barton fading for third, Euro Flyer takes fourth, Hester is fifth and Crystal Letters was never nearer.'

A breath I didn't know I was holding escapes from my lungs as Flash thunders past the winning post the rest of the field trailing in behind. Liv comes around to face me, grabs my shoulders as we scream and jump up and down on the spot.

'He bloody won!' she shouts. I smile on at a complete loss for words. We knew he was good, but that was simply breath-taking. Tom never moved, never changed his hands, never picked up his stick. He simply steered and stayed on board and let Flash's easy stride eat up the ground.

'Come on. We need to go and meet him at the gate.' I smile as I pull away from Liv's hysterics. We run down to the course gate, laughing fanatically. It reminds me of our childhood days running around the yard full of the joys of life. My heart beats erratically from the elation, relief and realisation of the superstar we have in our midst.

We reach the gate as Tom turns Flash back toward us. He must have been unable to pull him up.

'Emma, I'm speechless.' Laughs Tom looking down at me as we make our way to the winner's enclosure. 'He was incredible. That was no more than a piece of work for him.'

'I can't believe it.' I smile back.

A small hardy crowd gathers around the winner's enclosure leaning over the railing using their Racing Posts to shelter from the rain.

'Ladies and Gentlemen, please welcome in the winner of

our first race today here at Thirsk, Flashdance, ridden by Tom Doyle, trained by Emma Williams and owned by Richard Williams.' The pretty racecourse presenter announces to the crowd who offer a small but enthusiastic applause as we reach the winners stand.

Tom dismounts while Liv takes the reins over Flash's head. He envelops me in a hug and whispers in my ear, 'We did it.' I embrace him a little tighter.

'This is just the beginning.' I reply.

He releases me and pecks me quickly on the cheek before unbuckling the girth and pulling the saddle off while I pick up a bucket of water and offer Flash a drink, which he gulps down greedily.

'Gather round folks.' Asks the racecourse photographer. Liv pulls Flash around to face the camera and Tom comes to stand on his left, I stand with Liv on the right.

'Oh yes, gather around for a photo. You'll need the memory.' An all too familiar voice booms across the enclosure. My heart drops into the pit of my stomach. Daventhorpe.

He sidles toward us, brown fedora pulled low over his face. His rotund belly slows down his approach, but his sharp, malevolent gaze set within his chubby purple face pierces our perfect bubble. Tom grows a foot in height, and I can see his chest rise and his fists ball under the saddle and weight cloths. I rush over to him before he can make a move.

'Tom, don't. He's not worth it. You need to go and weigh

in.' I plead with him as I grab his bicep, hoping my words can break through the red mist that has so obviously descended upon him. He lets out a breath as he turns on his heel and high tails it to the weighing room.

'Horses away please. Weighed in, weighed in.' barks the steward over the loudspeakers. Liv, Flash, and the second and third-placed runners exit the winner's enclosure to cool off back at the stables.

I use this momentary pause to gather myself for the obvious confrontation that I am about to enter into.

'Lord Daventhorpe.' I address him before he can get the first word in. For all that he has put my family and me through, I will not let him get to me today of all days. I knew this was coming but I had hoped that maybe he possessed some shred of decency that would have made him stay away; that was naïve. Of course, he has to come here to cause one big ugly scene.

'You, young girl, have made a huge mistake.' He points a chubby finger accusingly at me.

'You have no right to be here. Please leave.' I dismiss him.

'How dare you speak to me like that. That horse is mine. I'm going to sue you for every penny he wins.' He spits

'He is not, you won't, and he never will be. I have the paperwork to prove it. Please leave.' I tell him again. The crowd leans further over the railing eating up the drama unfolding before them, pleased that this quiet midweek race day has got that little bit more exciting. The race sponsors shift uncomfortably on the presentation stand as they wait to present the trophy while instead, I spar with one of the most powerful men in racing.

He steps into my personal space as he tries to use his large build and booming voice to intimidate me. I take an awkward step back. Tom, now without his helmet, rushes out of the weighing room, colours untucked flowing around his waist.

'Get out of here.' Shouts Tom as he points at Daventhorpe who laughs sadistically.

'You have no idea what you've started. You better keep one eye open honey because I'm going to blow you out of the water.' He turns and waddles back off into the sea of people that have appeared from nowhere.

I feel breathless as the reality of his threat sinks in. None of us really knows what he is capable of. Tom pulls me around to face the sponsors so that we can finally accept our prize. Note to self *our* prize, *not* Daventhorpe's.

'Let's enjoy the moment Em. Don't let him spoil it.'

The race day presenter hurries over to us sheepishly. 'Are you ok to accept your prize now.'

I gather myself with a deep breath, 'Yes, we are thank you. Sorry about that.' She smiles and scuttles back to pick up her microphone.

'Ladies and Gentlemen, please put your hands together for Emma Williams who will accept the trophy on behalf of winning owner Richard Williams from sponsors Bet794 who have kindly sponsored this two-year-old novice event here at Thirsk today.'

I force a smile as I greet the group of sponsors gathered on the stand. I shake each of their hands enthusiastically and thank them very much for sponsoring the race as they present the silver horse-shaped trophy and champagne. We smile for the photographer. Tom comes up to join me to collect his winning jockey's prize, a small silver plate, and we pose for more photos. Despite Daventhorpe's best efforts, I savour the moment. Every winner is special and this one will stay with me for a long time.

'I'm going to go and see dad later.' I tell Tom as we disperse from the stand.

'Do you want me to drive you?'

'No.' he looks downcast at my dismissal, 'I want you to come with me.'

'To see him?'

'Yes.'

'Are you sure?' he asks a little taken aback.

'Yes, I want to tell him about our big winner.' I smile

'Ok, I'd love to.'

...

It is a little after six when we reach the care home, the sun has broken through the clouds and I feel lighter than I have in years. Training a winner, having Tom by my side, and my best friend back, I no longer feel alone. Hope fills my belly at what the future could hold knowing that my best days are ahead and not in the past as I had once thought.

Tom hangs back as we walk across the car park.

'Come on, he won't bite. It's not like he's your boss anymore.' I grab his hand and pull him beside me.

'Once a boss always a boss and if I'm with his daughter, he's definitely my boss.' He replies seriously.

'Oh shush. Are you that nervous about meeting the parents?' I chuckle

'Maybe a little.' He shrugs sheepishly.

'Hello Joyce.' I offer a little wave with my free hand as I continue to drag Tom along with me.

'Hello there dear. I hear congratulations are in order.'

'Aw thanks Joyce, they are.'

We make our way up the winding oak staircase and cross the carpeted landing to my dad's room.

'Wait here a second.' I whisper to Tom as I knock lightly on the white-washed oak door. As I do, I can hear a faint commentary coming from a TV somewhere. I poke my head quietly around the door and I see my dad sitting up in bed, the TV with the racing channel on is set up where he could easily watch it. When he sees me, he waggles his index finger at me as I enter the room and I am blinded by the most joyous smile I have ever seen grace his face.

'You saw it, didn't you.' I mirror his smile with my own, warmth fills my chest and my eyes begin to sting.

He nods the best he can, 'w… wi… n… ner.'

I rush to his side and give him the biggest hug I can, and he kisses my temple with a light but frail kiss. To see him so happy and to hear him speak for the first time in years fills me with unimaginable joy. I hug him and hug him and hug him enjoying the warmth only a father can offer their daughter.

'Daddy, there's someone I want you to meet.' I tell him as I pull back and look into his now bright, shining eyes. 'Tom…'

We both turn to the door as Tom creeps in sheepishly head slightly bowed. I stand from the bed as Tom comes to my side. Our closeness answers the question in my dad's eyes but he clearly recognises Tom showing that the strong and noble man I once knew as my dad has not all been lost or has been found again today thanks to our winner.

'Hello, sir. It's a pleasure to meet you.' speaks Tom tentatively.

Dad lifts both his arms in a gesture that tells him to sit down on the bed next to him and Tom duly obliges. He takes Tom's nearest hand and covers it with both of his in a sweet fatherly gesture, their eyes meeting in an affectionate stare. Emotion swells in my throat. Both men sit in a silent conversation that only those involved would know the contents contained within. One says I'm sorry for what happened. The other says I always believed in you and I'm glad you came back. Dad looks up at me and nods, giving me a silent blessing, letting me know he approves of Tom. I nod back and smile, placing a hand over my heart, unable to speak out loud.

He removes his hands from Tom's and lets him come to stand back beside me, as he does so, he gives him a little pat on the back of the head and points at me seriously. His way of threatening Tom should he do me wrong.

'Oh, dad. Stop it.' I laugh.

Tom pulls a pair of chairs from across the room so we can sit awhile. We take a seat and Tom places a tender hand on my knee.

'Did you see Flash daddy? Wasn't he amazing?' He nods enthusiastically, smiling at his trainer and jockey, 'He's gonna be a group 'orse isn't he.'

'P... pri...' he stammers 'ry... y... ou... n... eed.'

'What's he saying?' Tom whispers in my ear as dad and I stare deep into one another's eyes. We try to find clues to what he's saying in the deep depths there.

'Priory?' I question, and he nods

'The castle?' adds Tom. Dad nods again. Priory castle, Lord Daventhorpe's estate, just a few miles away from the yard. As quickly as he drops that bombshell on us, he changes the focus of our attention once again. He grabs my left hand and points to my ring finger while looking pointedly at Tom. Heat rises up my face in embarrassment. Talk about scare Tom off.

'Dad, stop it.' I laugh, but he just raises his eyebrows. I look over at Tom, who has gone a slightly paler shade of white but meets his stare right back and doesn't waver under the pressure of it.

'You guys. I'm right here.' I exclaim.

They eventually break from their staring match as dad holds my hand in his own. Tom and I chat a little while longer about the race, the horses and our options for Flash. Dad listens on intently. For the first time in years, he looks genuinely happy. Even before he had the stroke, he was always stressed, trying to please everyone and never really stopped, but now, here, with us together as a little family unit once again, he looks completely content. His happiness making me happy right there with him.

Before we leave, I give him a big bear hug wrapping my arms around him and burying my head in his chest while he gives me another kiss on the back of my head.

'I love you.' I breathe into him.

'I... l... ve y... ou.' He replies

I stand back up, and Tom moves over to shake his hand.

'I promise I'll look after her sir.' Dad nods at him seriously, then looks across at me and gives me a big goofy smile. My face can't contain my big cheesy grin, and I chuckle lightly at his antics.

We shuffle out of his room but before we reach the door, I look back and call out to him, 'Bye dad. Love you.'

Chapter Eleven

'That's the happiest I've ever seen him.' I tell Tom as we sit on the sofa in the living room of the trainer's house later that night drinking Flash's winning champagne.

'He was literally beaming.' He agrees, 'Em?'

'Yeah?'

'Where did the name Flashdance come from?'

I turn to face Tom, who sits on one end of the sofa, crossing my legs as I do and tucking them underneath me. Sam snores noisily snuggled up in a ball separating the two of us a big smile spreading across my lips.

'Well, I named him Flash as a foal because of his white blaze but then whenever we went to see him in the field dad would start singing that song from the film Flashdance you know the one? I try to sing the song very badly and we both start giggling, 'So after that, there was no going back, he was just Flashdance and it stuck.'

'I never would have put the two together.' He laughs, 'But I guess that kind of makes sense now.'

'You know…' I start, 'I feel like I know you but don't really know you.'

Tom raises a sceptical eyebrow in response, 'What do

you wanna know?'

'Your favourite colour.'

'Seriously?' he snorts

'Seriously.'

'Ok then. It's green.'

'Green. Interesting.' I stroke my chin conspiratorially.

'Ok then Inspector Morse. What's yours?'

'Purple. What's your favourite food?'

'Kiwi.'

'Kiwi!' I exclaim, 'That's so random. Out of anything you could have in the whole world, that's your favourite food? Please tell me you don't eat it with the skin on.'

'Ew no. Who even does that?'

'I've heard of people that do that.'

'You watch too much Youtube.' He laughs, 'And yours?'

'Chocolate cake.'

'Well, that's hardly surprising.'

'How?' my voice rises as I lean closer towards him, earning me a grunt from a snuggled-up Sam.

'Because I always see you eating it,' he chuckles.

'Fair enough.' I shrug. 'If you weren't a jockey, what would you be?'

'A rockstar.' We both laugh

'Really?'

'Nah, I don't know. I've always loved horses and I was always light, so I guess it was inevitable. How about you, what would you have done if you hadn't taken over the yard?'

'I don't know either. This is all I've ever known.'

Suddenly he turns serious, leaning towards me his darkening eyes zeroed in on my lips. I lean a little closer, allowing him to reach over and place his hand in my hair at the back of my head. We lean closer and closer towards each other like moths drawn to a flame. My heartbeat rockets and my eyes begin to flutter closed in anticipation. As we get closer, we forget Sam acts as a barrier dividing us on the old brown leather couch. He becomes trapped and startles awake as we begin to crush him. He hops off the sofa in disgust and waddles off to sleep in a safer place, probably by the Aga. We remain blissfully unaware of this as our lips meet in soft and tender caresses and I wrap my arms around his neck, eager to get closer to him. The kiss becomes more intense as he gradually deepens it. At that moment I was his, no longer in control, the rest of the world falls away, sparks ignite on the end of every nerve cell and no one else exists except us.

I open my eyes as we pull apart, drunk on the electricity that has passed between us. Tom looks as with it as me as we both catch our breath and wonder what has just happened.

'So, um…' I start

'Yeah, um.' Laughs Tom, 'I better go.' He shifts to get up, 'Early start in the morning and I haven't harrowed the gallop yet.'

'No,' I exclaim, 'wait a minute. I want to ask you

something.' He sits down waiting for me to start. 'Dad didn't scare you away earlier, did he?' I ask sheepishly, my cheeks turning a deeper shade of red.

'Em.' I fiddle with a nearby cushion. 'Emma, look at me.' I divert my attention back to him, 'I'm not scared. With you by my side, I am the happiest man alive.'

'Ok,' I smile.

'Ok.'

Our little cocoon of affection is shattered by the loud blare of my iPhone vibrating on the nearby coffee table. I reach across for it and my heart stops at the sight of the caller ID. The home.

'Hello.' I answer hesitantly dreading whatever it is the doctor needs to tell me at this time of night.

'Hello Miss Williams, it's Dr Lowther here. I am very sorry to have to tell you that your father has just passed away peacefully in his sleep. It looks like it was a heart attack, I'm afraid.' Everything stops. I hear nothing else and drop the phone to the floor. The walls crush me on all sides, my heart stops beating, my lungs cease to function, and my legs give way. I fall to the floor, landing harshly on my bum, but I don't feel the pain. All sensation has been lost other than the pain that sears through my heart. A tsunami of tears gathers at my eyes and I have no defences for it. It crashes out of me in one enormous, wretched sob.

I can't breathe. I can't speak. I can't move. I only feel pain. Pain in my heart, pain in my head and the wet, salt of tears burning down my cheeks.

'Thank you, doctor. Yes, I understand. I'm with her now… Yes, I can take care of things this end. Ok, goodbye.'

Tom must have picked up the phone and finished the call with the doctor. He sits next to me, pulls my head into his chest and gently strokes my hair as I sob uncontrollably into his shirt.

'Shh, it's ok.' He breathes into my hair as he places a light kiss there. 'I'm here, you just cry. Cry as much as you want.'

After a while, he wraps his arms under my legs and around my back, lifting me onto the sofa. He fits himself in behind me, wrapping himself around me, holding me, trying to put all of my broken pieces back together in any way that he can. What I can't tell him is that even in the brokenness of this moment, he completes me. Today my dad gave me his final blessing that it was ok to let Tom into my heart. The man that knew me the best in the whole world knew what I needed most and that was Tom. With him, I am just me. I don't have to be anyone else, not the big shot trainer, not the broken-hearted girl and most importantly I don't have to be lonely and even though my worst nightmare has come true, in this moment, I am not alone.

I feel his steady breathing fan across my face as we lie there in the darkness. The exhaustion of the day hits me like a freight train, my eyes grow heavy and I let sleep take me.

…

The next morning, I peel my eyes open to find myself lying alone on the sofa. I can't remember why I am laid here, why I am in yesterday's clothes and why does my head feel like I've been whacked with a baseball bat. Then it hits me like a blow to the stomach. He's gone. Tears threaten once again, and I sob quietly into the cushion placed under my cheek. Sam creeps into the living room, hops up and snuggles into my chest. I pull him into me and snuggle my face into his thick fur, inhaling his soothing doggy scent. Dogs have this innate ability to sense when you need them most and, in this instant, I love him more than ever before. Dad had bought him for me as a sixteenth birthday present and I'd immediately fallen in love. We are best buddies, completely inseparable and now he will always be a living reminder of all that my dad had bestowed upon me for my greater good.

This is the perfect, most heart-breaking sorrow. Only hours earlier my dad had been the happiest I'd ever seen him and even though he was so obviously disabled, I saw the old sparkle in his eye. He had seen me fulfil the promise we had made each other when we saved Flash from being shot by Daventhorpe. He'd said that one day that colt will be our saving grace. Shortly after, he had his stroke, but I never forgot what he said. He knew I was going to need him. Flash was our beacon of hope when everything else was falling into darkness.

After a while, my tears dry up and I lay in contemplative silence, enjoying the warmth and comfort of Sam the best

I can. Everything is raw, my emotions, my throat, my face from crying but at the same time everything is numb, and I feel like I don't exist, like I'm actually in some parallel reality. I always knew that one day this was inevitable but it still feels like a slap in the face, when yesterday we were so happy and full of hope and then, in a heartbeat, it is all ripped away and life deals another blow.

Tom tiptoes into the room, unaware that I'm awake, dressed in his usual yard clothes of brown britches and a dark wool jumper. He must have done the yard for me while I slept.

'Hey.' I start, my voice was raspy from crying.

'Hey. You ok?' He kneels down beside me and tucks a loose strand of hair behind my ear. My eyes start to sting again. 'Whoa come on.' He pulls me up so I'm sitting and kisses my forehead tenderly. I scrunch my eyes closed willing away another flood of tears. Sam hops down, happy to see Tom, who gives him a scratch behind the ear. 'You need a shower.' He announces. I groan and put my head in my hands, running my fingers through my now greasy hair. 'Come on.' He drags me upstairs and into the bathroom. I follow him limply. My legs feel like lead and I can barely hold myself upright. He flips the toilet seat down and instructs me to, 'Sit.'

Grief is a funny thing. It makes you question the very core of who you are, the decisions you've made and every single why and what if that's caused you to exist in this very moment. Why was he torn away from me so cruelly? Why does it hurt so much and what if the pain never leaves me?

'Em.' Tom speaks. I don't respond, lost in my thoughts and wallowing in the sadness that is beginning to consume me. 'Emma.' He raises his voice. I look up as he comes to kneel in front of me and takes both my hands in his, 'I know you're hurting right now, and it kills me too but would he want you to be sat here wallowing like this?' He looks right into my eyes and deep into my soul.

'I know.' I whisper. He squeezes my hands a little tighter.

'It doesn't make it any easier, but you said yourself that yesterday he was the happiest you've ever seen him. You have to take something from that.'

'I know.' I repeat, unable to formulate anything more complicated.

'Now, have a shower, you look like shit. It'll make you feel better. My mum always says a shower fixes everything.'

'What time is it?' I mutter

'One o'clock. Now come on and shower.' I can't believe I slept all that time. The yard must be finished by now.

'You're bossy. You know that.' I give him a look.

'Yeah, shower.' he replies indignantly and turns on his heel leaving me to get on with it.

I undress clumsily pulling my clothes off any way I can, not caring how tangled they become as they hit the cold tile floor. I climb in and let the hot water pour over my weary body as I begrudgingly wash my hair.

Sometime later, I make my way downstairs to find Tom, reading the Racing Post, sitting at the head of the table with Sam on his knee quietly awaiting my return. A mug of hot steaming coffee sits waiting for me on a coaster at the place next to him. I guzzle it down greedily, hoping it will alleviate the complete hopelessness that has overtaken me.

'Feeling better?'

'Yes, thanks. Sorry.'

'Do *not* be sorry.' He levels me with a heavy stare.

'Did you trot up Flash this morning?'

'Yep, he was sound as a pound and fresh as hell.' He chuckles.

'You know we should probably do a press release or something.' I reply, seeing the Racing Post in its usual spot on the table. 'I need to ring Liv as well and I suppose my god-awful mother.' I cringe inwardly at the thought of how that will go especially since I found out about her and Daventhorpe and the fact that I haven't spoken to her for at least two years since I took over the license when dad was first taken ill. Then we'd just ended up arguing about how she didn't care about her only daughter so I doubted she would care much now.

'I've already called Liv, she's at the firm until four and then she's going to come over and help us with all that but let's not dwell. I want to show you something.'

I follow him out into the yard, we don't stop in the barn and continue towards the fields and the broodmares. He tucks me into his side and wraps a supportive arm around my waist while I rest my head lightly on his shoulder. The early August sun is warming, and the wind swirls around us, making my hair flow around my shoulders. The swallows fly high and swoop low catching bugs while the sparrows sing from high in a distant tree. The sky is a vibrant blue and the clear day reveals the breathtaking view of the moors that my dad loved so much. Deep purple heather sits among golden hues of corn and moss green hills roll out for miles, eventually reaching the coast. The broodmares graze peacefully dotted around the paddocks swishing their tails occasionally while Legacy sleeps peacefully by the feet of Iron Lady, her small brown body just visible amongst the lush grass. The scene played out in front of us is the definition of peace and tranquillity and it makes my heart swell with gratitude.

'Why'd you bring me down here.' I turn to Tom as we lean over the fence, watching the mares.

'Because you needed it and I want to tell you a story that I think you will appreciate.'

'What is it?' I ask hesitantly

'It's not bad, I promise. It's about your dad.'

I don't say anything, just wait for him to continue.

'So when I was first here as a gangly, homesick sixteen-year-old your dad brought me to this spot. It hasn't changed one bit by the way. I was so lost I didn't have a clue what I was doing. All I knew was that I wanted to be a jockey. I'd packed my bags and my parents had given me their blessing to follow my dream to come over to deepest Yorkshire to train with the multiple group winning trainer Richard Williams. I made such a hash of things to start with.' He smiled to himself, 'I tacked up the wrong horse, went too fast when I was meant to be hack cantering, you name it I probably did it. Anyway, after a couple of weeks, I was ready to go home, and I think your dad sensed that so one morning, he brought me down here. He said to me, Tommy lad you've got talent in you son. I took a chance on you because you have something that cannot be taught and that's the love for it, but you'll never make it if you give up now. I just nodded like a robot absolutely in awe that he was taking the time to speak to me but then he said, look at that view. What do you see? I was just like um I see mares sir and a nice view but he said, 'No son, what you see is my legacy. Those mares will carry it on and give my little girl a future. You lad have got to decide what you want your legacy to be.'

A lump gathers in my throat and I close my eyes surrendering to my emotions. I could hear my dad in every word that Tom spoke. If I think back to that time, one of the mares must have been One Thousand Guineas winner Thatcher's Girl mother of Iron Lady and who's granddaughter Legacy now grazes the same paddock.

He edges closer to me, our cheeks aligned. 'Look Em, you did it. You're doing it now. There is his legacy, laid in that grass. Thanks to you.' I slowly peel my eyes open and absorb what Tom tells me. There is no need to be sad, just grateful. Grateful that he gave up everything to build up this place for me, grateful that he never stopped loving me and grateful that he hung on for so long and through so much pain to a time when he knew that I would be ok without him. He always taught me that after death comes new life and I had to grasp the one I had been given because it was my life to live.

'Hey, Tom. Why'd you come back?'

'Because it felt right, you know. Sometimes life puts you on a path you never thought you'd walk, and you have to trust it enough to find out where it's going to lead.'

I pull him into a hug, wrapping my arms around his muscular shoulders and bury my face into his neck, 'Thank you.' I breathe. He replies by hugging me tighter and not letting me go.

...

Sickness settles on my stomach as the phone line buzzes on and on interchanging between tones.

'Hello?' the nasal voice of my mother breaks through the chorus.

'Mum, it's Emma.' I breathe deep trying to remain calm and not wanting my voice to crack.

'Emma?' her voice rises, 'What is it?'

'It's dad. He died.'

'Oh.'

'Oh, is that seriously your response?' A jolt of anger

ripples deep inside me.

'Well, you always knew it would happen one day, Emma.'

'How can you even say that?' I screech down the line.

'Well, it's the truth. I don't know what else you want me to say.'

'Oh, I don't know. I'm sorry or are you ok or how about when shall I book my flight for the funeral.'

'I'm not coming to the funeral.' She states matter of factly seemingly oblivious to how upset I am.

'I don't understand you. Do you not even want to be there, if not for him then for me?'

'No, you don't understand.' She squawks, 'I am very sorry for your loss Emma, but I simply can't come back. I've been away a long time Emma; I know you and your father were very close, but you'll be fine, you always have been. Now I have to go so I'll speak to you again sometime. Goodbye.'

She ends the call and I'm left with only the mocking buzzing of the phone line for company. *Oh yes, mother do call again sometime, and we can decide how much of a shit parent you want to be today.*

I fumble back into the kitchen at a loss for words where Tom and Liv sit waiting for me to sort out all the legalities. Thank goodness for best friends who are lawyers.

'How'd it go?' winces Tom when he sees the expression on my face

'Fabulous.' I seethe

'So, she's off the list for the funeral then.' Adds Liv.

'She refused to come so yes you could say that!'

'Stone cold.' Replies Liv shaking her head in disbelief, 'Enough funeral talk for now. You need to decide on a press release before they do it for you.'

'Just put something like group winning trainer, long illness, I've taken over, private funeral, thank you, the end.' I hated the press and how they spun stories, so this was the last thing I wanted to do right now even though it was probably the most important.

'Don't worry Em. I've got this.' She smiles and gives my arm a quick squeeze before setting off typing madly at her laptop.

'I've got you something.' Whispers Tom as he leans across the table. He pulls out a white paper box from the fridge and grabs a fork on the way back to the table. He places them both neatly in front of me.

'What's this?' I chuckle

'Open it and find out.'

I carefully peel back the top layer to reveal the most enormous piece of chocolate fudge cake. Despite the cloak of sadness that still surrounds me, a wide smile spreads across my face.

'Did you make this?'

'I'm talented at many things, baking is not one of them. Clare sorted it out for me and sent those flowers over there.' He points to a beautiful bunch of lilies placed on the countertop.

'Aw, thanks.' I say before digging my fork into the gooey chocolate and filling my face with as much as my mouth will take. Tom shakes his head in disbelief as I wolf down my drug of choice.

'Ok guys I've finished.' Announces Liv as she slides her laptop across to me to read over, it is perfect.

'Thank you.' I tell her as I give her a big warm hug before she makes her way home, leaving Tom and me alone in the kitchen.

'I better go too. That cottage won't heat up itself.' Tom breaks the silence as I bend down to give Sam a belly rub.

'No.' I exclaim, 'Please stay. I don't want to be alone.'

'You'll never be alone.' He whispers into my ear as he pulls me into an embrace and grips the back of my head protectively. 'Never.'

Chapter Twelve

The ability to procrastinate has always been a skill of mine, today I am fully exercising this ability. The day of the funeral has arrived and to say that I don't want to deal with it is the understatement of the century. No one enjoys funerals, they are an event that you just have to get through to appreciate a life lost and to move on with the one you still have. Dressed in a lace, knee-length black dress and heels with my hair half up, half down, I drag my feet around the living room, putting off the inevitable. I know Tom is waiting for me in the kitchen, but I need some time to myself to gather my thoughts and emotions in readiness for the inevitable difficulty of today. I make my way around the room perusing the various winner's photos and trophies displayed on mantle pieces, shelves and walls. I drag my finger over a bronze statue of a galloping horse, brushing the dust off its back. As I ponder, I feel my father's presence with me. A small feeling of him stood beside me in solidarity and in strength igniting an inner fire within, a simmering flame that would fuel me through this day, letting me know that I would get through this.

I find Tom standing peacefully in the kitchen, back

against the wall, head pressed upwards, eyes closed in quiet contemplation. He looks magnificent in his black tailored suit, shoes shined, his soft brown hair styled into place with a small strand escaping onto his forehead. The finishing touch to his outfit is a red and blue striped tie, my dad's colours. Could this man be any more perfect I think to myself as I take him in, his chest rising and falling slowly as he takes a moment to himself.

'Hey.' I announce my presence softly.

'Hey.' He replies, opening his eyes slowly and taking a final deep breath. 'You look stunning.'

'I was going to say the same to you.' I glance down at my feet, a little embarrassed, heat rising slightly in my cheeks. I walk to him so that we are standing toe to toe and pick up his tie, 'I love this,' I say. 'Dad would be so proud.'

'I didn't just do it for him,' he answers taking the tie from my fingers and bending down slightly so that we're eye to eye, 'I did it for you too. So that everyone can know that I'm all for you and that I always will be.'

His admission chokes me up. I am unable to speak for fear of crying again. I place a hand over my heart and meet his deep blue gaze through my tear-stained eyes in a silent thank you.

'Come on, we better go.' He says as he places a tender hand on the small of my back and leads me from the kitchen.

…

The service is beautiful and gives dad a perfect send-off. The fifteenth-century church is partially filled with a carefully selected congregation of dad's closest friends and old racing contacts. The stone pillars are adorned in white roses, the ancient architecture and intricate stained-glass windows give a sense of majesty to all those who enter within the sacred walls. Tom and Liv sandwich me in the front pew lending me their strength and warmth and anything else they can offer to get me through the service. Afterwards, as we file out into the cobbled streets of Wharton, I feel completely drained, numb to my core and ready to sleep for a year. Despite the sad day, the sun peaks through the clouds as I try to mingle with some of the guests, shaking hands, making small talk and reminiscing about dad's greatest moments.

'Thank you for coming.' I say shaking the hand of Giles Maher.

'I wouldn't have missed it for the world.' Replies the former jockey and one of dad's oldest friends, one that he would often sneak off to the pub with, much to mum's disgust. The short and stocky man, now in his late sixties, shakes my hand decisively with a small sympathetic smile before making his way down the street to his parked car. He limps slightly making his shoulders seem lopsided and slowing what would have otherwise been a brisk pace. I look up to meet the familiar blue-eyed stare of Tom who has finished chatting with a man I recognise to be a former trainer and old friend of dads. Our staring match across the small crowd is interrupted by a familiar, petite lady of about sixty years, she had kind green eyes and curled grey hair.

'You probably don't remember me,' she starts. Her voice triggers a memory and I instantly recognise her as our former housekeeper, Viola.

'Lola. It's been too long. Thank you for coming. I really appreciate it.' I answer earnestly as I step forward to embrace her. She wraps me in a tight hug, stroking my hair affectionately as it cascades down my back in unruly curls. Her endearment and warmth take me back to a time when she was the absolute centre of my universe. I wouldn't go to sleep unless she read me a bedtime story, not even dad would suffice. A wave of emotion washes over me at the memory, even though she was just our housekeeper, she was so much more. I never truly understood why I felt such a strong pull towards her, maybe it was because my mother was so cold and indifferent towards me.

'You've grown into such a beautiful young lady. He would be so proud.' She says as she pulls back, still holding onto me, appraising me in comparison to the little girl she once knew.

'Thank you. Have you retired now Viola? I still miss your amazing cakes.' I smile. She returns my smile with her own, turns to a bag behind her and pulls out a white paper box.

'I thought you might say that, so I brought you a little something.'

I open the lid to find a mouth-watering chocolate fudge cake topped with shiny ganache and her signature strawberry.

'Thank you so much, it looks amazing. Come and visit the yard anytime I'm sure the house would be happy to see you again. I can't say I look after it half as well as you did.' I chuckle, shaking my head.

'Oh, I'd love to lovey but it's hard for me to get away, though I shall definitely try.'

'Do you still work for Lord Daventhorpe?' I say the words slowly still at a loss for why our once beloved housekeeper went to work for the most objectionable man in the north of England.

'Um, well, no.' She seems a little flushed, 'But that's a story for another day, I must go, unfortunately. I am running late, goodbye now.' She hurries off, her floral skirt floating in the breeze as she goes.

'Viola, wait!' I shout after her disappointed that she has to leave so soon, 'Come back to the Winning Post with us for some food.'

'I'm sorry lovey. I must go.' She turns briefly, pausing to look me up and down one last time, but doesn't halt her exit.

Why was she so flustered when I asked her about Daventhorpe? She must have left us about five or six years ago but I can't pinpoint why she did. Another mystery caused by Daventhorpe no doubt, the man left a trail of destruction wherever he went. I loved her like a mother, she was always there for me and seeing her here today makes me miss her more than I have in a long time.

'Was that Viola?' breathes Tom into my ear as he wraps

his arms around me from behind, his chin resting on top of my head. I instinctively lean back into him.

'Yeah it was but she got all funny when I asked her about Daventhorpe.'

'Strange I always thought she never liked him.'

'She brought me cake though so I guess we can forgive her this once.' I try to lighten the mood.

'So, if I ever do something wrong, I can just bring you cake and you'll forgive me.'

'Maybe. Maybe not.' I grin.

'Come on lovers we gotta go.' Shouts Liv from behind us.

Tom and I break apart linking hands instead to walk the short way to the car.

…

When we arrive at the Winning Post, an enormous spread of food awaits us. A few of the invited guests have stayed on and mingle making small talk with each other. Viola is long gone but old Giles Maher remains and chats with another former jockey I recognise, both small in stature but large in personality.

'Wow, they really know how to put on a spread at this place.' Liv states in awe as she grabs a plate and begins filling it with sandwiches and cakes. At the sound of her admission, Clare enters the restaurant from the bar, greying blonde hair flowing around her shoulders as usual.

'Anything for this girl.' She wraps me in a motherly

embrace.

'You shouldn't have.'

'Nonsense.' She bats me lightly on the head as she pulls away. 'Eat up.' She gestures to the table with a sweep of her arms, turning on her heel to oversee the lunchtime service in the bar.

I was too nervous to eat this morning and my stomach rumbles in protest at the sight of all the food, from sandwiches to quiche to croissants to cupcakes, there is enough for twice the people here. I grab a plate and start filling it with a few sandwiches, a chicken skewer, some salad and a chocolate cupcake before pulling out a chair next to Tom and across from Liv at a nearby table.

'So, seeing as this is a sad day I think we should exchange funny stories about your dad.' Announces Liv between mouthfuls. 'I'll start. One day I came around and we were sitting in the kitchen chatting and your dad came in on the phone. He was having quite a heated conversation to some cold caller I think it was and he was like, will you stop ringing me I haven't had an accident and If you don't stop ringing I will... I will call the stewards. With that, he hung up. You said to him, dad don't you think you should have picked something more threatening like the police and he was like well it was the only thing I could think of.'

'That sounds like dad.' I chuckle lightly at the memory.

'Tom, what about you. You must have a few?'

Tom smiles down at his plate, pushing his food around

with the back of his fork.

'I arrived at the yard at about the same time as another lad, James. Mr Williams told him his first lot was Gremlin, the pony and he actually believed him. He tacked up the fat little welsh pony in all his brand new racing tack and pulled him out into the yard with all the other lads riding around waiting for their instructions. We were all killing ourselves laughing and your dad tried to keep a straight face, but he was a goner when he saw him. He said to him, James, I like you lad, I think you'll do well here and then fell about laughing with the rest of us. The poor lad went bright red, he was absolutely mortified.'

'He never told me that.' I get out between belly laughs.

'Then he said you might as well take him up the gallops now and then…'

The old oak door creaks open halting Tom's story and my laughter. I see his shadow before I see him. His large frame and beer belly struts into the restaurant. All chatter stops and the pub is sustained under a blanket of silence commanded by the presence of the honourable Lord Daventhorpe. A jolt of anger shoots through my system ricocheting from the top of my head to the tip of my toes. The red mist settles upon me and I curl my fists. How dare he show his face here. Tom starts to rise from his seat before I do but I grab his shoulder and push him back down. I can deal with this.

'This is a private function.' I launch the chair back into the floor and march over to the tweed suit and fedora clad

Lord Daventhorpe.

'Don't flatter yourself I didn't come here for the egg sandwiches.' His smarmy face raises in a smirk as he stands on the threshold of the restaurant.

'Show some respect.' Tom races to my side. The anger practically boils off him, shoulders raised, muscles tensed, and fists balled at his sides. Lord Daventhorpe rebuts him with another smarmy grin.

'Well, what a sad day this is indeed.' He feigns sympathy, 'But *this* has come to my attention.' The blood drains from my face.

'Excuse me what on earth are you talking about?'

'This will come out tomorrow in all national newspapers.' He hands me a brown envelope. I pull out a draft of a newspaper article.

Lord D in financial scandal at the hands of the late Richard Williams

One of British horseracing's most powerful and revered owners has revealed that he is owed £250,000 by the late Richard Williams who is said to have stolen the money during the sale of King George winning sprinter Priory Castle. The exciting homebred colt caught the eye of an anonymous Australian buyer after his scintillating win back in 2015 but was subsequently sold for an undisclosed sum thought to be in excess of £1 million. Lord Daventhorpe has revealed he plans to take legal action against the estate of

Mr Williams in order to reclaim what he is rightfully owed. 'This has come as a great shock to me.' Lord Daventhorpe told the paper, 'I am extremely disappointed to have learnt that my trusted trainer was in fact just a common criminal. If the funds are not repaid in full, I will have no choice but to take legal action.'

I can't read on, my stomach sickens at his words. I slowly look up to find Lord Daventhorpe smirking as he readjusts his fedora to sit perfectly central on his chubby purple face.

'You're a piece of shit.' Snarls Tom who must have read the article over my shoulder.

'This is complete fiction. Where is your proof?' My voice rises an octave as I battle to stay calm. How dare he tarnish my father's reputation when he is no longer here to fight against his lies. 'You didn't need the money then and you don't need it now, so go back to your pit of lies and leave us the hell alone.' I screech. A slow, deep laugh breaks from his belly.

'I don't need the proof girl. The only person with a pit of lies is your father and as the executor of his will, you now owe me what was stolen.'

Tom launches towards him, ready to strike him across his double chin. I anticipate his action and grab his arm, pulling it back down across my chest. He looks down at me, eyes wide, the anger pumping in his veins. Don't. He's not worth it. I say, with my eyes.

'Seeing as you're… how shall I put this… skint, I am

going to make you a one-time offer.' He interrupts our silent conversation. 'Hand over the colt who is rightfully mine and I will write off the debt owed.'

'Lord Daventhorpe. You never fail to surprise me.' I start with a fake smile, 'But you're sick in the head if you think you will ever have any claim over him.' I seethe

'Get out of here you disrespectful pig.' Shouts Tom

'Oh, you've hurt my feelings now.' He places a hand on his heart and starts to laugh sadistically to himself. 'But in case you're tempted to enter him in any further races you'll want to see this.' He hands me another piece of paper.

'What is it?' I don't bother to give him the pleasure of seeing me read it.

'It's a draft of the email I will send to the BHA disputing the ownership of the colt which will inevitably lead to an embargo on all race entries, movement and will force the sale of him at public auction. So it's 250K or the colt. The choice is yours.' He finishes with a smirk, turns on his heel and struts out of the pub.

'You're completely deluded.' I shout after him as the oak door crashes closed with a thump. I scrunch up the document. Tom pulls the ball from me, halting the assault from my frustrated fists. 'I need to sit down.'

I blink and then blink again. Am I alive? Am I dreaming? Unfortunately for me, the answer to both questions is yes. Liv, who has been observing our duel with Daventhorpe, comes to my side and drags me back to the table. She pulls both the papers from Tom and starts to read over them herself.

'I'm sorry to interrupt but I wanted to wish you well before I left.' Giles stands behind me an arm outstretched ready to shake my hand.

'Thank you, I'm sorry about all the commotion.'

He gives me a sympathetic nod and turns to leave along with the rest of the guests, judging by the emptying restaurant.

'We need to go.' Tom stands up abruptly, causing the chair legs to screech along the hardwood floor. He comes perpendicular to my side and starts to guide me towards the exit. Liv gathers the papers and scurries after us following us to Tom's waiting truck. We all pile in, in haste, Tom has the engine fired up and starts to pull out before I can even get my seatbelt on.

'Tom, slow down. If you let him get to you, he wins.'

He replies with a grunt, fists balled around the steering wheel, knuckles turning white. I turn away from my observations of Toms angry state when my phone starts to buzz in my bag. I pull it out to find an unknown number lighting up the screen.

'Don't answer it.' Tom grinds out continuing to shift uncomfortably, his jaw ticking

'Hello?'

'Hello, this is Clive Jenkins from the Racing Post. I am calling about the…'

'Hello, Mr Jenkins I know exactly why you're calling, you are Daventhorpe's pet reporter, aren't you? Tell me how much does he pay you to print his bullshit?'

'Um… well… um.' He stammers, clearing his throat, obviously put on the back foot.

'I have absolutely nothing to say other than that these allegations made against my father are completely and utterly false and furthermore I think you should show a little respect calling me on the day I buried my father. So you can go tell your paper I'll be filing a court order for harassment if you ring me again.' On that note, I hang up. My heart is racing and I blow out a long breath. I hated confrontation and I hated that Daventhorpe had chosen this day to spout these lies. I knew today would be hard, but it should have been a day to give thanks and remember the wonderful man that my dad was, it never entered my head that an allegation like this would be brought against him. It is easy to worry about what a day will bring and how you will cope if something bad happens, but I was completely dumbfounded as to how we would get through this.

…

Tom, Liv and I sit around the kitchen table, papers strewn across it, staring blankly at each other at a loss for how to react to Daventhorpe's bombshell.

'I don't believe this for one second.' I state emphatically, 'Dad would never take a backhander, he was always straight down the line.' The other two remain silent, 'Guys?'

'I don't know Em. I'm sorry.' Speaks Liv with a sympathetic stare.

'So you believe him?' I feel a jab of hurt. How could she believe he would steal that much money and from Daventhorpe no less?

'No, no. I'm not saying that but if he produces some form of proof you have a serious problem that's all I'm saying.'

'He's kicking me while I'm down.' I drop my head in my hands in despair and rub my face in frustration. 'I mean let's all be honest I don't have that kind of money lying around, so it's either sell Flash or sell the yard.' Panic rises in my chest and I get up and start to pace, I could not lose everything my dad had singlehandedly built up.

'Em stop. This is ridiculous, there must be something we can do.' Tom grabs my arm on my third lap of the room, sitting me back on the chair next to him. 'Why's he only bringing this up now? He had absolutely no need to sell that horse to Australia and surely he hasn't just found out today, even if it is true.'

'You're right. As absurd as it sounds, he's waited for this, for him to die, to create this big charade. There's got to be another reason, we have to fight back. I will clear dad's name if it's the last thing I do. I will not stand by and let him destroy us.' I slap the table for emphasis, causing Sam to jump out of a deep sleep by the Aga.

'What are we gonna do?' Tom says, leaning back in his chair, 'We don't have a clue what crap he's going to pull next quite apart from the fact that we may not be able to run Flash, our one shot at the big time. The way he won the other day I thought straight away that he should go to the Racing Post Trophy.'

'Ok, one thing at a time.' Liv replies.

'We're so screwed.' I shut my eyes in defeat. Then it hits me, dad saw this coming. 'Shit.' I shout.

'I can't tell if that was a good shit or a bad shit?' questions a very confused Liv.

'Shit.' I repeat.

'Em what is it?' Tom looks at me with wide eyes.

'Tom, remember when we went to see dad. What did he say?'

'Shhiiittt.'

'Exactly, he must have known this was coming.'

'Guys what are you talking about?' asks an increasingly exasperated Liv.

'When I took Tom to see dad on the day Flash won, he started speaking, only one and two words at a time, but he said you need Priory Castle.'

'Ok.' She answers sceptically, 'I don't follow. You could argue that means he did take that money.'

'Liv, stop being such a lawyer and have a little faith in humanity will you.' I bite back, 'We need to get inside the castle. There must be something there that either proves dad's innocence or helps us prove his sole ownership of Flash.'

'It's got to be worth a shot,' agrees Tom, 'but how are we going to get inside?'

Chapter Thirteen

'I can't believe you talked me into this.' I stare at myself in the mirror, trying to recognise any part of my identity. Dressed in a gold sequined flapper dress with a low back, fishnet tights, killer heels and long black gloves I could have stepped off the set of the Great Gatsby. My long ginger curls are concealed under a black bob wig and feathered headband with dark eye makeup and red lipstick finishing off the look.

'You look hot and duh that's the idea.' Scolds Liv who has chosen a dark green velvet knee-length, long-sleeved evening dress with waterfall fringe detailing that fans down her legs. Her usual long blonde waves are styled into a short blonde updo with silver bangles and an oversized pearl necklace that reaches as low as her stomach completing her outfit.

Daventhorpe's annual pre-Ebor meeting party, a Great Gatsby 1920s extravaganza is being held at Priory Castle tonight. All the bigwigs and who's who of the racing world will be at the strictly invitation-only event. Despite the many years we trained for Daventhorpe, I have never been to his pre-Ebor party. Dad never let me go when I was younger and then I never wanted to go when I was expected to attend.

Last year Robbie went stag and I dread to think what he got up to in a room full of drunk people in fancy dress.

'How do you even plan on getting us in. We're not invited.' I ask, trying to pull my dress lower towards my knees, unhappy with how exposed it makes me feel.

'*You're* not invited. *I,* on the other hand, have an in.' She announces while finishing off her makeup.

'You have an in?' I raise a sceptical eyebrow and hop onto the windowsill for a sit-down.

'What's that you said to me the other day? Have a little faith.' I fix her with a questioning stare, not convinced. 'Put it this way, I know the guy on the door.'

'How do you know the guy on the door? Do you know him well?' I waggle my eyebrows at her.

'I just know him, ok. Ask no questions, when we get there, follow my lead.'

'I don't know why I'm friends with you.' I laugh

'Shut up and stop moaning. We've got a party to crash.' She drops her mascara back into her makeup bag and drags me off the windowsill. 'Tom's going to have a heart attack when he sees you.' And with that, it's her turn to waggle her perfect eyebrows at me. I turn a deep shade of red as I try to pull away from her.

We find Tom waiting in the kitchen standing with his back toward the Aga, eating a bowl of spaghetti, Sam is curled up next to his feet. When he sees me, he stops the fork halfway between his mouth and the bowl. His mouth falls open, the long-forgotten pasta falling limply back into the bowl. I pause in the doorway, a little embarrassed, I didn't like to stand out at the best of times, to be dressed like a flapper girl was *way* out of my comfort zone. Liv strides over to a dumbstruck Tom and pats him on the right cheek, 'You're welcome,' she says and goes out to the yard.

'Wow.' He breathes, placing his bowl onto the sideboard. I walk over to him, keeping my eyes down in a bid to hide from his stare, my heels clicking on the stone floor. 'You look absolutely incredible.' He smiles at me, placing both hands on my exposed back our bodies pressed flushed together. 'I don't think I can let you go out alone dressed like this.' He chuckles, his eyes darkening. 'You sure I have to be the getaway driver? I think I need to be there to beat off all the men with a stick or maybe a baseball bat, whatever works best.'

I chuckle and shake my head at his macho antics. 'Stop looking all lusty at me and yes you need to be our getaway driver.' We agreed last night that Liv and I will go into the party as we can dress up and hide our identities much easier. Then we will make a quick getaway through the back of the castle to Tom parked in a secluded lay-by.

'You literally have no idea. No idea.' He tightens his grip around me.

'Come on we've got to go. No sex on the table.' Shouts Liv from the yard and I groan at her crassness.

'Now there's an idea.' Ponders Tom.

'Focus. This is serious, we've got a job to do.' I push him away playfully gathering the truck keys off the table while Tom follows me begrudgingly out of the house.

…

'Remind me again how you know this door guy.' I whisper into Liv's ear as we teeter across the gravel courtyard to join the queue of eager guests in front of the imposing Palladian style house that is Priory Castle. The dramatic façade and six columned front entrance with stone staircases rising up to it from each side sparks grandeur yet fear into all who dare enter between the spiked iron gates guarded by black stone falcons who sit high on the gate posts. If approached on a dark night, you could expect to see lightning strike above the grand house, however, tonight the soft hum of jazz music diminishes the somewhat cold and garish feel of the estate preventing the usual shiver that runs down my spine whenever I have been forced within these walls.

'Just follow my lead.' She whispers. 'Jamie.' She purrs as she approaches the clipboard holding door steward. He is the definition of tall, dark and handsome with nearly black hair, high cheekbones and a perfect white smile. He leans down to give her a fond kiss on the cheek that lasts a little longer than is comfortable for those watching and continues to whisper something in her ear that makes her blush and giggle. Someone clears their throat behind us in the queue. She jolts away from him, reaching a hand behind her, searching for me until she eventually manages to grab hold of my arm.

'This is my girl Lucinda.' Jamie smiles across warmly at me and gives me an appreciative once over. My cheeks heat and I shift uncomfortably under his stare, he is handsome, but I am taken, very taken.

'Have a good night ladies.' He nods and gives Liv a knowing wink before turning to address the other waiting guests.

'Do I want to know.' I ask Liv as she pulls me into the grand hall.

'I don't think so.' She swallows and offers me a sheepish grin.

As we enter the grand hall, I am dumbstruck. On this occasion and this occasion only, I have to hand it to Lord Daventhorpe, the party oozes the glitz, glamour and scandal of the roaring twenties. Women are dressed in all forms of 1920s attire from flapper dresses to ball gowns adorned in oversized jewellery and garish headdresses while the men are clothed in lounge suits of varying colours of tuxedos. Waiters dressed in white tailcoats serve champagne while the jazz band plays from a raised platform at the far end of the hall. The lead singer clicks his fingers to the beat while he serenades the guests with Let's Misbehave by Cole Porter.

'You heard the man. Let's misbehave.' Shouts Liv above the music, pulling me onto the black and white dance floor. I spy Daventhorpe standing on the balcony above the hall, smoking a cigar overlooking the party below. His large frame is squeezed into a tuxedo; what's left of his black hair oiled flat onto his head. The sight of him makes me sick to the stomach. 'Relax no one will recognise you.' Liv adds as she attempts to do the Charleston swivelling her left then her right foot in front of the other and waving her arms over her head for a little more authenticity. I try a little swivelling of my own, but it is much harder than it looks. In the end, we both fall about laughing, grabbing each other's shoulders gasping for air.

I look up to the balcony where Daventhorpe remains smoking his cigar. Liv follows my gaze sobering up from our antics. We are here to do a job and get out as soon as possible to avoid detection. 'He's nothing on Leo, is he?'

I roll my eyes in reply to that joke. 'Come on, the drawing-room is down that corridor.' I point to the left of the hall and start to make my way towards it trying to look as inconspicuous as possible while Liv follows close on my heels. We make it to the entrance of the dark corridor, a white rope hangs across it with a private sign suspended in the middle. I look back to make sure no one is watching us before I crouch underneath it. Liv follows and we start to tiptoe into the darkness trying to keep our heels from clacking on the polished stone floor. I keep a watchful eye behind us, making sure we are not being followed. My heart races at the thought of being caught and we are not even in the drawing-room yet.

'Clary, you're overreacting. It was nothing I swear.' A frustrated male voice shouts from up ahead.

'Shit is that Robbie?' Whispers Liv. With my back pressed against the wall, I feel around for a door handle, closet or cupboard in the darkness of the corridor, anything that we can hide in. If Robbie finds us here, it's game over, finished, the end and all this will have been for nothing.

'Here.' Liv drags me into a nearby storage closet. We stand face to face, a sliver of air between us as we try to fit into the small space, my back is pressed against a stack of shelves and I think I can feel a mop next to my right foot.

'It was nothing, was it? That's why you were in our bedroom with two brunettes on either side of you.'

'Oooooh shit.' Whispers Liv into the gloom of the closet. We are so close I can feel her breath fan across my face. My heart lurches at the accusation against him. I never had any reason to believe that Robbie had cheated on me, but it did cross my mind that it was entirely possible and that made a little bile rise in the back of my throat.

'It's not what you think. They were fully clothed.'

'Oh and that makes it all the better does it, the fact that they were fully clothed, because guess what, it doesn't.' She screams

'Clary come on. I still love you,' he pleads half-heartedly.

'I think I just puked in my mouth.' Snickers Liv, 'This guy is getting kicked in the balls tonight.'

'You don't love me, you've never loved me, you're just a gold-digging, career-obsessed, half-wit, who loves no one but himself.' She shrieks. 'And I hate your hair, it makes you look like a toilet brush.'

'Yes, girl, yes, give it to him straight.' Liv whispers and I have to hold my breath to contain my laughter. I am starting to like Clarissa, she is saying all the things I'd wanted to when Robbie broke up with me. I silently urge her on.

'Clarissa stop it you're embarrassing yourself let's just go and enjoy the party.' He implores

'If you think I am going to be paraded around on your arm like some accessory then you can forget it. You're only with me to get the ride on my dad's horses, well guess what I hope he fires your skinny arse and sends you hopping down the road.'

'She's got a point, he does have a skinny arse.' I giggle into Liv's ear who clings onto my shoulders enjoying this drama a little more than she should be.

'You think I'm the half-wit.' He sneers. 'Your daddy will never fire me. I'm too good, I win races and I know too much.' He jeers. Urgh, Robbie is such a jerk. I know it. Clarissa knows it, and everyone knows it but unfortunately, he is probably right. Daventhorpe would never risk any of his scandalous secrets coming out into the public domain but it is our job to do just that. We just have to wait until these two finish the soap opera in the corridor.

'I hate you.' She screams with a loud huff and stomps off up some stairs, the walls ricocheting as she goes.

'Women.' He groans, 'I need a drink.' He clomps past our closet hideaway and hopefully out to the glitzy party, most likely to select the next notch for his bedpost. We wait in silence as he passes and then for a little while longer just to be safe. I feel around in the darkness, searching for the door handle, finally landing on it and slowly opening the door. I poke my head out into the dingy corridor and repeatedly blink, readjusting my eyes to the slightly brighter environment.

'Is it clear?' Liv whispers, still in the cupboard

I scan the periphery for any potential threats to our plan to raid Daventhorpe's drawing-room. There is no one that I can see but whatever lies concealed in the shadows of this dark back corridor, I dread to think.

'All good.' I reply

She nudges me out of the cupboard and we skate our backs down the wall keeping one eye in front and one eye behind as we make the final steps towards the bulky oak door that guards Lord Daventhorpe's hallowed drawing-room, and all the secrets that we hope are contained within. With one final glance behind I turn the ornate brass handle and tentatively creak open the door, peeking my head inside. Liv bundles in behind me as I assess the room.

The oak-panelled seventeenth-century drawing-room has two large, floor to ceiling windows dividing the back wall. Hanging between the windows is what looks like a Stubbs painting of a striking grey horse standing in a bleak landscape. Another painting of a woman hangs above the marble fireplace where a small fire crackles. Why there is a fire lit on a mild-August night, I am unsure. A brown leather sofa is placed in front of the fire adjacent to an ancient oak desk while the far-left wall is covered in shelves of first edition books and aged brown folders.

'You take the shelves, I'll take the desk.' I decide

Scurrying over to the desk, I kneel down and try some of the drawers. I heave at the intricate silver handles but to no avail. Locked. I try the drawers one by one on the right-hand side of the desk. Locked, locked and you guessed it locked. The desk itself is spotless, only a fountain pen and a crystal paperweight decorate the otherwise plain oak top.

'Come on.' I groan, trying them again, this time with a little more force. 'Liv you got anything?'

'No. Who's that?' she replies.

'Who?' My heart lurches, I hadn't heard anyone come in. I stand to attention fearful we are about to get busted and pull my dress down.

'That.' She points above the fire to a half-length portrait of a woman, her long blonde hair fans down her back and her piercing blue eyes stare straight into my soul, a small yet knowing smile painted on her lips, she is beautiful.

'That's the late Lady Daventhorpe, I think.' I try to drag her out of the depths of my memory she had died when I was very young.

'Well, it certainly makes sense where Clarissa gets her looks from. What happened to her?' She replies, gazing up at the picture in awe.

'Car crash, I think. Daventhorpe was heartbroken if I remember rightly, nearly sold up he was so grief-stricken.' Liv breaks her gaze from the painting and raises a questioning eyebrow at me. 'Hard to believe I know, but she always seemed like a kind woman, how she ended up with Daventhorpe I'll never know.'

I gaze at the painting a little longer appreciating how realistic the work is. If Lady Daventhorpe stepped out of the painting, I would not be at all surprised. My eyes roam lower to the fireplace and the roaring fire contained within it. In between the swirling orange hues are pieces of paper that singe and curl under the assault of the flames. I step around the sofa in a bid to get closer, straining my eyes trying to read any of the text.

'Hey Em, come look at this.' Liv is bent over the coal bucket unfolding a load of scrunched up papers inspecting each as she goes. 'Bingo.' She smiles. I lean over her and read the paper as fast as the letters will form in my head. At the head of the paper, FINAL DEMAND is printed in big red letters. Below the letter from the bank outlines that his multiple loans have remained unpaid for three months and if efforts to repay them are not made in the next month the bank will have to take further action including the possibility of foreclosure. Liv passes me the paper and delves back into the bucket.

'These are all final demands Em. If this isn't a motive for coming after you, I don't know what is.'

'Will you still love me?' *Gulp,* 'When I'm no longer youuunnngg and beauooootiful?' A very out of tune and slurring Robbie warbles as he clomps down the corridor directly towards us.

'Oh, gees.' Sniggers Liv, 'We need to get out of here pronto. Here.' She hands me one of the final demands shovelling the rest back into the bucket, 'I'll distract him. Hide behind the curtain until you hear us go, then use the window and wait for me with Tom. Ok?'

'Ok.' I scurry on my tiptoes to the nearest floor to ceiling red velvet curtain and wrap myself in behind it while Liv makes her way to the door trying to look as inconspicuous as possible.

'Hey babe, you lost? I don't think you should be down here.' He leans in the doorway, crossing one foot in front of the other.

'Oh, um yes I was just looking for the loo.' She smiles sweetly.

Liv is clearly putting on her best ditsy blonde act. Robbie is dressed in a light pink lounge suit and boater. He holds a tumbler of whiskey in his right hand, swirling the ice cubes around with intent.

'Oh my gosh, you're Robert James, aren't you?' She skips over to him, brimming with excitement.

'Yeah babe that's me but please call me Robbie.' He smiles his whitest most alluring smile puffing out his chest and jutting his hip out further.

'I've always wanted to meet you. You're like the best jockey ever, right?'

'I am pretty good, not gonna lie. Can I get you a drink? A pretty girl like you shouldn't be wandering alone in dark corridors.'

What a corny chat-up line and *I am pretty good not gonna lie,* who does he think he is? God's gift to racing? What did I ever see in him? I ponder my life choices while watching my ex-boyfriend chat up my best friend who is doing her best jockey-hopper fan-girl impression while I impersonate a curtain. Everything has gone to shit, it's official.

'Dark corridors come on. Are there a lot of dark secrets hidden around here then?'

'You have no idea babe no idea.' Through the tiniest gap in the curtain, I watch as he places a hand on the small of her back, leading her out of the drawing-room and towards the party.

'You're so mysterious, I love a bad boy.' She giggles.

The sound of their footsteps diminishes as they go. I take a deep breath. One, two, three, four, five. I can't hear anyone else lingering in the corridor, I gently unwrap the curtain and peek my head out, thankfully my only company is the still cracking fire. I step over to the window and, using the ancient brass handles, heave up the bottom pane. I flip off my heels and toss them out first, then with one more backwards glance I hop on the ledge and out onto the manicured grass lawn below. I turn and pull the window shut so that Daventhorpe has no reason to grow suspicious, pick up my heels and leg it down the drive in my stocking feet.

Breaking into ancient houses and crashing Great Gatsby parties is amazingly liberating. As I sprint down the old cobbled drive doing my best to avoid loose stones, I feel more alive than ever. I can see Tom's truck tucked into a lay-by up ahead hidden by the longstanding pine trees that line the ascent to Priory Castle. I rip open the back door and throw myself onto the seat completely unable to contain my smile. Tom jumps to attention spinning around in his seat, having obviously prepared to wait a lot longer for my arrival.

'Jees…' He starts, 'Where's Liv?'

'We kind of got hijacked by Robbie and she had to deflect him while I escaped through a window.'

'What did you find?'

'Well, not a hell of a lot other than final demand letters from the bank. They were scrunched up into balls in the fuel bucket next to the fire that had papers burning in it.'

'So, there's our motive. What now?'

'I'm not sure.' I reply, feeling a little deflated, 'I guess we wait for Liv who is hopefully avoiding being mauled by Robbie.' My cringe is mirrored by Tom who rolls his eyes in disgust.

'That guy is a creep.'

'I know right?' Liv shouts as she bundles in next to me. 'However, when it comes to drinking, he is a complete lightweight.' Tom fires up the engine and high tails the truck down the drive and out onto the road.

'And?' I prompt trying to fasten my seatbelt.

'Well, you heard him tell me pretty girls shouldn't lurk in dark corridors which is cheesy as…'

'Liv.' I interject before she can go off on a tangent.

'Right.' She pauses. 'He invited me upstairs and took me into a bedroom. He was swaying around and trying to undress but I managed to keep him on the other side of the room. I distracted him by asking him about all the antique furniture when I stumbled over a shoebox that was half under the bed. I tripped over it and hundreds, maybe even thousands of fifty-pound notes fell out all over the floor. When he saw what had happened, he went crazy and started shouting. He was like get out you stupid bitch don't you dare steal my cash. He slammed his mouth shut as soon as he said it, but he said it all right. He's been receiving dirty money and I think we all know from who.'

'But I thought he had no money.' I question out loud.

'He has no money in the bank. He must be dealing in cash at the moment but what has he been paying Robbie to do?'

'Stopping horses, it's got to be.' Tom interjects as he drives.

'Seriously? Do you really think so?' I ponder in reply.

'Yep, I do.'

'That's all well and good but how are we going to prove any of this. All we have is crumpled demands from the bank and that's not exactly a crime.'

'One step at a time Em. One step at a time.' Liv places a supportive arm around my shoulders, and I lean into her side. We are well and truly onto him, we just need something or someone to help us prove it and put Daventhorpe away once and for all.

Chapter Fourteen

It is a brisk morning in late September, I eagerly watch the horizon, binoculars set to my eyes, waiting for Tom to breeze Flash up the gallop. The early morning mist drifts low over the ground soaking the grass in dense dew and the sun spears through the clouds in golden forks. I tuck my chin into the collar of my coat in a bid to escape the cool autumn air while Sam snuffles around in the undergrowth and inspects a giant white toadstool.

Black shadows appear on the bottom bend and I focus in on the advancing figures. Flash eats up the ground, his hooves hit the woodchip in perfect rhythm, sending the pieces flying up in his wake. His breath rushes from his nostrils in long streams forming clouds in the cold air around him. The early morning light hits his luminous bay coat and his black mane flies around his neck as he lowers and raises his head. Time stands still, he turns into the final straight and the mist parts as he makes his ascent creating an almost dreamlike scene in front of my eyes.

'Whoa yeah.' Tom hollers as he flies past and I let out a loud laugh. That was amazing. I jump in the truck lifting Sam in with me, fire up the engine and drive up to meet the pair at the top of the gallops.

'What do you think?' I call out to Tom, trying to contain my smile, as I drive alongside him and Flash, while they walk back down the gallop after their morning breeze.

'Awesome,' he beams, patting Flash on the neck. 'So awesome. He's the best two-year-old I've ever sat on Em, I mean that. We have to find a way around Daventhorpe because this horse can win the Group One at Doncaster next month, mark my words.'

'As soon as he passed the post at Thirsk, the Racing Post Trophy came straight into my head.' I confess.

I continue to drive alongside them as Flash swishes his tail and clears his nostrils. Sam claws his way onto my lap and pokes his snout out of the window.

'I'll meet you back at the yard. Liv's coming over to sort through some old documents.' I announce as I accelerate away.

…

'What are we looking for?' I question Liv as we stare at the rows of old filing cabinets and boxes that gather dust at the back of the office.

'Contracts, emails, letters, horse's files, staff files, bank statements, message books, diaries, bills, receipts, address books, phone books.'

'Got it.' I chuckle, 'it's going to be a long day.'

I take the filing cabinets while she makes a start on the boxes and we set to work painstakingly sorting through twenty years' worth or more of paperwork.

'There has *got* to be more to the Priory Castle saga then meets the eye.' Liv comments as she brushes the dust off a dog-eared filing box.

'I know, I can't stop thinking about what dad said, maybe we've got it wrong maybe he didn't mean the place, Priory Castle, maybe he meant... oh I don't know. We just have to keep looking.'

We sort in silence for the next half an hour. I sift through pages and pages of records, emails and staff wages. My eyes sting from scanning the text and my index finger throbs from a paper cut I was yet to get a plaster for.

'Damn it, we're never going to find anything.' I flop onto my back from where I'm sitting cross-legged on the floor.

'Do you know if you kept old training bills.'

'Why?' my heart lurches in hope, 'What have you found?'

'As per the training agreement section 17.2 states that once an invoice is outstanding and unpaid for more than one month after delivery, a Trainer shall be entitled, on the expiry of 21 days' notice to the Owner, sent by recorded delivery to the Owner's last known address, to dispose of one or more of the Owner's horses and apply the proceeds towards all unpaid invoices, keep of Owner's horses during the period of retention under the lien and all other costs including the reasonable costs of valuation pursuant to the clause 17.3 and the costs and expenses of sale.'

'What are you saying, that's standard practice.'

'What I'm saying is Daventhorpe owed you money when he took the horses right?'

'Yes.'

'So, you could argue that you have taken ownership of Flash against the debt owed to you by Daventhorpe.'

'But he doesn't own him.' I argue

'No, not technically since he is registered to your dad but if Daventhorpe did produce a document proving he has a claim to him you could use this line of argument.'

'I see where you're coming from, but Flash is worth five times what he owes me.'

'But that's what I'm saying what he owes *you*. Some of those final demands were years old, which could mean he owed your dad a hell of a lot more than he owes you. We just have to prove it.'

I move to the next filing cabinet, hoping to find some old training bills or aged debtors lists. I heave open the metal draw and flick through the plastic name cards. I reach the file squeezed into the back of the cabinet and wrench it forward, trying to read the name card on it, but it is blank. I pull out the unassuming brown paper file and open it up. The first sheet of paper lists ten horses that I recognise to be Lord Daventhorpe's.

East Cliffe
Kissing Gate
Clary's Girl
Yorkshire Gunner

Dunkirk

Trumpeter

Spitfire

Graceful Sophie

Incredible Isabella

Galileo Ex Priory Princess colt

The last horse on the list makes my heart leap out of my chest. There is only one Galileo colt I know of, and that is Flashdance. The list is void of a date but the fact that Flash is still unnamed makes the list about two years old and dated it to just before my dad got sick. I quickly flick to the next page searching for some context to link the list of horses to something, a bargain, a deal or contract. Instead, I find a handwritten note,

Richard,

As requested,

Collect as discussed.

Debt considered paid as per contract

Silas Daventhorpe

PS – This is to remain strictly confidential, any word to the press and the deal is off. Burn both documents once read.

'Yes.' I shriek, jumping up and down

'What the…' You scared the bejesus out of me, Liv blows out a breath.

'Read. This.' I practically chuck the file at her.

A wide conspiratorial smile spreads across her face as she inspects the file, 'This is perfect.'

'Flash is officially ours.' I beam, 'And he must have known dad never put him down like he had told him to.'

'It looks like more than Flash is officially yours judging by this list.'

I ponder that thought for a minute. Daventhorpe must have monopolised on dad's ill health and gone back on his word to exchange the ten horses for the outstanding training fees. I feel stupid and naïve for not knowing about the deal, especially when Daventhorpe had bullied me into running horses like Dunkirk when he had no right to. I guess that was the level of deception he was willing to create to keep up appearances. Then there was Demelza who I had sold in a bid to keep the business afloat when Daventhorpe withdrew all his horses without paying his outstanding bills. If he was so skint, where had he found the money to buy her and where was she now? An ache settles in my chest I still feel horrible for selling her but at the time I had no other choice.

'What do I do now and what about the 250K he's threatening me with? He'll hit the roof when he knows I know about this and let's be honest he's not going to willingly let me have those horses. *Oh yes Emma, here you go, I will honour my secret deal with your father please have ten of my best horses.*'

Liv closes the file and takes a seat in a swivel chair, 'That's something that you and Tom will have to decide on. I can help you legally, but we need to be careful as we still don't know if he's filed a suit for the Priory Castle money.'

'How's it going girls?' Tom comes into the office, Sam at his heels. 'Wow, how many dead trees have you got in here.' He laughs inspecting the mounds of papers piled in various corners of the office. 'What's wrong?' He asks when he sees my conflicted expression.

'Do you want the good news or the bad news?'

'The good news…'

'Dad made a secret deal with Daventhorpe just before he had his stroke exchanging ten horses, including Flash and Dunkirk for his outstanding training fees.'

'That's amazing news. So, we don't need to worry about his stake over Flash anymore. What's the catch?' He leans against a desk folding his arms.

'The letter was meant to be burnt and never spoken of again. Plus, we can't exactly turn up with the horsebox demanding those other horses add in the fact we have no idea if he can prove that we owe him 250K.' I let out a ragged breath, falling into Tom and placing my head on his chest. He wraps his arms around me and rubs my back soothingly. I am relieved we have found something as close to concrete as possible, proving he has no right to Flash but what he will do when he finds out that we all know, scares me. He is a very powerful man and can pull a lot of strings when he has a vendetta against someone.

'I don't know what to do. I don't want to provoke him.' I talk into his chest, squishing my eyes closed in confusion while his hand, in a gentle circling motion, rubs my lower back.

'Em, I gotta go. I've got a case I have to work on before tomorrow. Call me and let me know if you want me to set anything in motion.'

I look up and turn from Tom's hold, 'Thanks so much Liv, see you later.' I smile.

I turn back to Tom and meet his gaze with mine, 'What do you think?' I ask tucking my head under his chin.

'I don't know.' He stares blankly into the distance, 'But I think we need to sit on what we know and keep it quiet for now.'

'Ok.'

...

After a quick lunch, I make my way back to the office to tidy up all the papers and most importantly, to lock away the folder with the letter. I turn the silver key in the lock and give the top drawer a tug making double sure that it is locked before hiding the key under the potted plant by the trainer's desk. I head into the yard ready for evening stables appreciating a break from the mountains of paper we spent the morning sorting. As usual, Flash is the first to greet me, nickering softly as I enter the barn, I stroke his face up and down his white blaze and look into his eyes. I will never understand how anyone can abuse a horse when they so willingly give us everything expecting so little in return. I love training, and winning races has an undeniable and incomparable buzz, but I love the horses first.

The bond I share with Flash runs deeper than any other horse I have ever encountered because he seems to know that I have saved him but also being with him and looking into his dark brown eyes makes me feel closer to dad. I hope he is in a better place, but I know a small piece of him remains here in the yard watching over us and probably rolling his eyes and shaking his head at my decisions.

My thoughts are interrupted by my phone, buzzing in my pocket. Another unknown caller lights up the screen and I deliberate whether to answer it or not. I know Tom hates it when I answer random calls because he doesn't trust the press.

'Hello?' I give in to the incessant buzzing.

'Emma Williams?' A deep male voice answers.

'Yes.

'This is Lawrence Kent, I am Lord Daventhorpe's lawyer. It has come to my attention that you are filing a suit against my client for the seizure of ten horses.' A shot of adrenaline courses through me and rises up my back. How does he know? How does he know already, and what am I going to say to this pompous ass lawyer?

'What firm are you associated with?' My voice rises, and I swallow, trying to keep my composure.

'Kent, Clifton and Dapper.' I instantly recognise the name as the competitor of the firm where Liv works. 'Now Miss Williams I must warn you most firmly that this will not come of anything and that as I speak my associate is filing a counter-claim against you for the seizure of the horse…' some papers shuffled in the background, 'Flashdance.'

My resolve snaps. I am done. This arsehole is about to find out what it feels like to piss off a redhead.

'Do you know what Mr Kent, you can do what you want because I am done with Lord Daventhorpe's shit. I am done with him dictating my decisions and most of all I am done worrying about it. I know for a fact that you have no hard evidence but guess what, I do. So see you in court.' I cut off the line without giving him time to respond. My heart and mind races, what have I done?

I immediately dial Liv. I can't believe that she would go ahead and file a lawsuit without my say so. I don't know how I would forgive her if she had. I force that thought away and dial again. Still nothing.

Frantic, I run around to the storage barn where Tom is moving around the hay in readiness for the new batch that is due to arrive. Covered in sweat, he is wearing a navy vest top, dirty blue jeans and brown work boots while hauling small hay bales from one side of the barn to the other. Watching him all hot, sweaty and dirty I momentarily forget my panic.

'What is it?' He drops the bale he is carrying and comes over to where I stand in the entranceway.

'Daventhorpe, he knows.' I run a ragged hand through my hair.

'What! How?'

'I don't know, it must have been Liv, but I don't believe

she would go to him without my say so. His lawyer rang me just now and said they were filing a counter-suit to own Flash outright.' The volume of my voice rises as I speak.

'Was it an unknown number?' Tom squeezes the bridge of his nose between his thumb and his forefinger.

'Yes.' I huff

'Bloody hell Em what have I said about answering unknown calls.' He exclaims in frustration.

'Why are you blaming me?' I shout back

'Well, I'm not the one who just gave away our best shot at ending Daventhorpe's hold over us.'

'You don't know that I gave anything away.'

He laughs humourlessly, 'I know because I know you. You're a hothead and when someone comes at you, you go at them twice as hard.'

'I'm sorry you think so.' I shout back, frustrated and turn on my heel hurt at his words.

'Em, wait, calm down. You know that's what I lo…'

'Don't even finish that sentence.' I snap, 'You're not about to say the L-word in the middle of a fight.'

'Em come on. You're being hot-headed now. You need to calm down and we can talk about this logically.'

'No, what I need to do is go to work so I can earn some money, so we don't go under.' I screech, turning on my heel, anger pulsing through my veins. I know I'm not thinking straight but I need some time alone to think. I get back to the house, change and get my keys as quickly as possible. I'm not truly angry at Tom, but I am angry at the situation, angry at the possibility that Liv has betrayed my trust and angry at losing the pull we thought we had over Daventhorpe. Tom was right, I am a hothead, but I don't feel ready to let him know that. I am a redhead, what does he expect?

When I arrive at the Winning Post for my shift, I have only calmed down a little bit. Adrenaline still courses through my veins and I fight to keep my breathing even and facial expression as close to neutral as possible rather than the raging bitch face I am trying to keep at bay.

A familiar gnarly face approaches the bar, 'Smithy.' I state bluntly, 'What can I get you?'

'Pint.' He states in his usual gruff voice. I plonk it on the bar with a thud trying to ignore the stench that radiates off him, a mixture of alcohol, body odour and another smell that reminds me of mouldy cabbages. If I think about it too much, I will retch so I turn away as quickly as possible and busy myself reorganising a pile of menus.

'There's something wrong.' Clare states coming up behind me cashing some change in the till.

'What?' I question turning around, 'Where?'

'No, there's something wrong with you.'

'Oh.' I drop my eyes away from her, 'Tom and I had a fight.'

'And you said something you regret?' she prompts.

'I snapped at him and I wish I hadn't.' I reply ashamed.

She fixes me with a sympathetic stare putting her hands

on my shoulders, 'Never leave a loved one when you're angry.' I open my mouth to reply but she leaves me with that piece of wisdom and hurries back to the kitchen to place an order.

As I serve other people, I can't help but feel a set of eyes watching me. I look up to find Smithy's stare fixed on me from a table in a dark corner at the back of the pub. That guy gives me the creeps, there is no doubt about it and he certainly seems to have it in for me. My whole-body shivers but I try to shake off the feeling of unease that settles over me.

My mind switches to thoughts of Tom. I want to get home as soon as my shift finishes and apologise for rearing up at him when I know he only wanted what was best for me.

By half ten the pub is beginning to clear out and I persuade Clare to let me go early. I let myself out into the cold night, the black sky covers those below in a dark blanket trapping the cool air below the clouds. My breath fogs around me and I fire up the engine of my car, turn the heating up to full in a bid to get warm, put my headlights on and pull out of the car park.

I reach the final junction that leads onto the main road that runs back to the yard. I look left and right out of habit, checking for traffic even though I can see no lights in the distance. I point my toe to press the accelerator but as I am about to make contact an unimaginable force crashes into me. The entire car ricochets and the right-hand side crumples around me. My head hits the window with a loud smash causing my teeth to clack against each other and an indescribable searing pain radiates around my head. A trickle of blood rolls down my cheek to my chin and drops onto my trapped legs. My right leg is ensnared in the wreckage having been directly in the firing line of the other car.

I try to wiggle my toes, but I can't, the agony is too much. My eyes roll back in pain and shock swells in the pit of my stomach. I can see a flickering light and then a brighter one shines into the car, but I can't open my eyes wide enough to focus on it. A putrid scent meets my nostrils and bile rises up my throat. What is that smell and why is it familiar? The light disappears and I am cloaked once again in darkness. I try to scream, shout or feel around for my phone but I can't move, I am trapped and there is no escape.

It is in this moment, as life slips away from me that I admit to myself that I love Tom. I love everything about him from how he calls me out on my overthinking to how he loves the horses as much as I do. If I ever get the chance to start this life over again, I will tell him that sooner. I love him, I love how he makes me better, I love everything that we have built together, and I love that I have a future that I want to share with someone and that someone isn't just anyone, that someone is him and only him. Why have I only realised this now? I am never going to be able to tell him face to face that I love him more than anyone I had ever thought I loved before. As I lie alone in the steaming wreckage, I pull his face to the forefront of my consciousness and picture his deep blue-eyed stare, his soft brown hair and sharp cheekbones. I picture him next to me, telling me that it will all be alright, that we can get through this as we have before, but I don't believe him this time. From this moment on, I never want to live without him. How cruel it is that he will have to learn to live without me.

Chapter Fifteen

The wind rushes through my hair, sending it flying around my shoulders. I grip Flash's mane wrapping the coarse black strands around my fingers and point my toes to the floor for security, clamping my bare legs around his body. My long, white lace dress cascades over his quarters and swirls behind us as he gallops. The grass rushes by in a blur, the ground reaction force passing through his limbs jolts through me and I hold on tighter.

The rhythm of his limbs increases and he gallops faster, faster, faster, the wind rushes harder still and the tears fall quickly. When had I started to cry? I lean forward into his mane and wipe away the salty droplets. He accelerates his pace once again. When I look up my heart lurches in my chest, we are heading for the edge of the cliff. He doesn't steady, doesn't shy away, he has no fear. As we near the edge, I wrap my arms around his neck and bury my face in his mane, then he jumps. I brace for the impact of the fall, but it doesn't come. The world disappears and we are flying, soaring high above the clouds. But I am losing my grip. The strength leaves my hands and I can't hold on anymore. His mane falls through my fingers and I slip from his back. Now

I am falling, falling faster, faster, faster. I am plunging ever downward and I lose sight of him.

'Flash.' I try to scream but my mouth and throat are too dry to resonate a sound. I slip through the layers of clouds and gasp for air. I attempt to stretch out my arms to break my fall, but I am restricted. A sharp pain jolts up my left arm and my head throbs. Beep, beep, beep. Beep, beep, beep. Beep, beep, beep. It is dark once again. Flash is gone, the clouds are gone, the light has gone. But why am I still falling?

'Em, baby, stop struggling. I love you; I love you so much please wake up, stop struggling.' A voice pleads. My eyes search for the light, my ears focus on the voice and the weight on my shoulders. With a colossal effort, I force my eyelids to part. I am greeted by an ashen-faced, dishevelled and red-eyed Tom who pins my shoulders gently to the bed.

'What are… ow.' My whole body aches, my head feels like it's been struck by a sledgehammer and I can't move my right leg. 'Where am I?' I ask, confused, my voice raspy and hoarse. Tubes, wires and machines connect to all parts of my body and my left arm is fitted with a cannula that nips and pulls at the tender skin. He drops his hands from my shoulders, placing a breathtakingly tender kiss on my forehead. He leans back meeting me with his perfect blue-eyes I've come to know so well.

'Tom? Where am I? Where's Flash I fell off him when he went over the cliff?' I cast my eyes around the white-walled room, unable to move my neck for the uncomfortable plastic brace that is restraining me.

'You're in hospital. Dear lord Em I thought I'd lost you. I've never been so scared in all my life.'

'But how?'

'You were in a car accident.' His voice drops to barely above a whisper, like he can hardly bear to say the words aloud. I focus on his beautiful, melancholic face and search for memories of a car accident.

'But... I was riding Flash and he jumped off the cliff and then we were flying but then I was falling, and I can't remember anything about a crash what happened?' I ramble feeling panic rise inside me.

'Shhh.' He tucks a strand of hair behind my ear, 'Flash is fine, it was probably just a dream.'

'What happened to me?' He takes a deep breath as he glances away from me. 'Tom?' I question again.

'You were in a hit and run. Someone hit you on purpose as you were about to pull out onto the top road. You have a head trauma, broken your leg and...' he trails off unable to continue.

'And what?

'You had internal bleeding and had to have surgery on your liver and spleen and then...'

'What Tom, just tell me!' I try to raise my voice frustrated with his inability to disclose what had happened to put me in this hospital bed.

'You needed a blood transfusion.'

'But who? I can't. Did mum come over?' I ramble. I was in an extremely rare blood group meaning that if I ever needed a blood transfusion, it had to be from someone with the same type. I had never thought much of it when I had found out as a child, thinking I would never be in the position to need a transfusion.

'They found someone.' He looks away, a guarded expression covering his face. I see straight through it and want answers.

'Who?'

'What do you mean who?' he asks incredulously with a shrug of his shoulders and a forced smile.

'Who?' I set him with a heavy stare.

'Viola.'

'Viola!' I exclaim, 'But how, why, I never knew! Ow, my head hurts.' I wince in pain.

'Shh, it's ok.' He starts to stroke my hair again. 'You don't need to worry about that now. I'll go tell the nurse you're awake.' He leaves me with another sweet kiss and a longing glance before exiting the hospital room. A few seconds later, a brown-haired nurse with kind eyes comes in to see me.

'Hello sweetie, how are you feeling today?' She moves over to the drip and monitors and records my levels on a clipboard.

'My head is pounding, my stomach hurts, I can't move my leg and this neck brace is cutting me in half.'

She meets me with a sympathetic smile, 'I'm not

surprised lovey you've been through the wringer and given us all quite a fright. I don't think your husband has eaten for a week. The doctor will be in soon to check your surgery site and hopefully take your brace off.' I stop listening when she mentions the word husband, but I'd been in here a week? That seems impossible.

'I've been asleep for a week?' I question.

'You were rushed into surgery as soon as the helicopter arrived as they needed to stem the internal bleeding. Plus, you took quite a bang to the head! The doctor was worried about a bleed on the brain but thankfully the latest CT came back negative. You're one lucky lady, not to mention that lovely husband of yours. He hasn't left you for more than a second from the moment he ran into the ICU. When you're feeling better you really must change your name I think it has a lovely ring to it.' She smiles widely.

'Sorry.' I reply, 'This is a lot to take in.'

'I know lovey you just rest now, and the doctor will be in shortly to adjust your pain meds.' She drops the clipboard into the slot at the end of my bed and leaves me to the many questions that whirl around inside my head. When did Tom and I get married? How did I end up in a car crash? Why does everything hurt so much and where is Tom now?

As I start to wonder where he is, Tom pokes his head around the door. 'Don't be mad.' He has the modesty to look a little embarrassed. 'They wouldn't have let me in if I hadn't told them we were married.' He comes over and squishes himself onto the bed next to me. He crosses his legs, placing a warm arm around my shoulders and kisses the top of my head. 'I'm just… I thought I was going to lose you the way they were talking. During the hell of this last week, I realised that I never want to be parted from you. I can't be parted from you, you complete me. I love you Emma. I'm so in love with you that it hurts.' His voice wobbles and I fight back the urge to cry for fear we will both start to sob.

His confession of love for me makes me forget all the pain that radiates throughout my body. I pick up his free hand and kiss his palm, 'I love you too.' I croak, 'But just for the record, you didn't force me into marriage while I was unconscious?' I chuckle.

'No.' he titters, 'When I ask, I want to hear you say yes.' On that note, we settle into contemplative silence and I snuggle into his side the best I can while constrained by a drip, a neck brace and a broken leg in a cast.

The doctor comes in a little while later to examine my stitches. He shines a light in my eyes, asks me a few questions which I try to answer as sensibly as my brain will function and thankfully, he removes my neck brace.

'I must say you were extremely lucky that we could find a blood donor when we did. I am concerned about your memory loss, but we can monitor this. The police are waiting to talk to you whenever you can help them with their investigations but until you feel ready, I will keep them away.'

'Thank you, doctor.'

'Hey, Tom.'

'Mmhmm.' He murmurs from where he has returned to his position snuggled next to me.

'How did...' my eyelids grow heavy, 'How did... Viola know?'

'Shh, just sleep for now.'

The sky is dark overhead, so I switch my headlights onto full. I pull up to the junction and set the car to pull out but I can't, my limbs don't work. I look up and see Dad, Tom, Liv and Viola standing side by side on the top road bathed in the beam of approaching headlights. Why are they stood there? They need to move, or they will get hit. I reach over to open the car door, but it slams into me and the whole car crumples. My head smashes into the window and I am thrown into the steering wheel. I search the road for them, they stand and watch as the blood trickles down my face. 'Help.' I wheeze but they remain unmoved. Lights are approaching. A car approaches. They're going to get hit they need to move. I try to move my limbs once again, but I'm trapped this time and there is no escape. A putrid smell of alcohol surrounds me. I try to close my nostrils to the smell but there is no escape. The lights get brighter as the car comes into view, it accelerates, their eyes remain on me, but they do nothing. 'No!' I scream as the car comes into view the engine roaring. 'No!' I brace for the impact, but it doesn't come. Darkness surrounds me once again. I am alone, trapped in the wreckage with no escape. My eyes search for the light but I fall further and further into the darkness. 'Help.' I wail, 'Somebody help me!'

I jolt awake and gasp for air, 'Tom!' I yelp frantically searching for him on the bed with my arms.

'I'm here. I'm here.' He leaps up from the bedside chair and strokes my hair tenderly, trying to calm me down.

'I remembered the crash.' I snivel as a tear escapes down my cheek which he wipes away with the pad of his thumb. 'I was coming back from the Winning Post. The car hit me and then there was a light and I smelt this awful smell of alcohol, but I recognised it. Smithy was there. I could smell him and …' it hits me like a bullet that the last time Tom and I spoke before the crash we were fighting. 'Oh my God, Tom, I'm so sorry.' I sob, 'The last time I spoke to you I snapped at you and I'm so sorry, I'm so sorry.'

'Hey, that's enough. Do you think I care about that? You can shout and snap at me all you want. Just promise not to scare me like that ever again, ok?'

'I'll try but Tom, it was Daventhorpe, wasn't it? It was, wasn't it?' I babble.

He meets me with a sad stare and nods his head slowly, 'I'm beginning to think so.'

'I'm scared.'

He hops up on the bed beside me and cradles my head in his arms, 'I will never let him or anyone hurt you ever again.' He replies fiercely.

I attempt to form a smile, 'I love you.'

'I love you too. Now try and get some sleep. I'll be here when you wake up.'

'Promise?'

'Promise.'

Chapter Sixteen

I wake up the next morning to the sound of strained voices from outside my hospital room. I wiggle my fingers and toes out of habit and move my head from side to side. I'm breathing, I'm alive but good lord my entire body hurts.

'Liv she's still asleep. You need to chill out.' Tom mutters

'But I need to see her, check that she's alright. I'm going crazy here Tom, this is all my fault.'

'Liv, stop.' He retorts. 'You can speak to her later but for now, that will only stress her out and the doctor said she has to be kept as calm as possible.'

'Tom she's not Mrs Doyle yet, you're not her gatekeeper. Let me in there or I'll go snitch that your marriage is about as kosher as an illegal immigrant's.'

Their heated conversation evokes memories before the crash. I remember discovering the list Daventhorpe had left to my dad. How he must have known for a long time that we had kept Flash rather than putting him down as he had ordered. I remember answering the phone to Daventhorpe's lawyer who threatened to counter sue for Flash if we tried to make a claim for the remaining nine horses. I remember questioning how he found out and desperately calling Liv through fear she had betrayed me to Daventhorpe.

'Tom?' I shout, trying to get his attention. He lets out an audible sigh and I visualise him running a frustrated hand through his slightly wavy brown hair.

'I'm coming Em.' He replies before pushing through the swing doors hurrying towards me in long strides. 'How are you feeling?' He asks perching on the edge of the bed.

'A little better, I guess. Tom?'

'Yes.'

'Is that Liv out there?' I reach up fixing his ruffled hair.

'Sorry, did we wake you?' he grimaces slightly.

'I want to see her. Can you send her in.' I sip at a glass of water, trying to alleviate my raspy throat.

'I will if you're sure.' He frowns but I nod anyway, 'Liv.' He calls and she replies by peeking around the door.

'Hey.' I encourage her to enter. She looks completely dishevelled, pale as a sheet and like Tom, looks like she's been wearing the same clothes for the last week.

'Em I'm so sorry this is all my fault I feel completely responsible.' She rambles as she scurries over to my bedside. Tom runs a frustrated hand down his face and neck, obviously troubled by whatever she is about to reveal. 'How are you feeling? How can I make it up to you? I'm so sorry.' She continues.

'Liv.' I interrupt her, 'I'm fine.'

'You're not fine.' Tom interjects not meeting my eyes to which I set him with a hard glare.

'Now pull up a chair and tell me what happened because I have literally no idea what has gone on this last week.'

She drags a plastic chair to the opposite side of the bed to Tom and sits down with a flop, her shoulders sagging. She looks up, sighs and begins. 'So, when I got back to the firm that afternoon, Daventhorpe was waiting for me in my office. I don't even know how he got in or how he knew I worked there; he must have found out about us gatecrashing the party. I had a stack of papers under my arm and he grabbed them from me, and they fell all over the floor. Unfortunately, I had taken a copy of the horse's list when we were in the office and he immediately recognised it, picked it up and ripped it in two. He said he was going to make you sorry that you ever crossed him and that if I wanted to get home safely that night, I wouldn't tell you.' Her voice cracks and she can't bear to meet my eyes. Tom's mouth is fixed in a tight line and his jaw ticks. 'I'm so sorry Em, I never thought he would actually try.' Her eyes begin to water, and she fiddles with her fingers on her lap.

'It's ok.' I pass her a tissue in an attempt to console her.

'No, it's not,' Tom retorts. 'You lay dying in a car wreck because of him. I watched you... I watched you cling on...' his voice breaks and tears threaten to spill out of his already bloodshot eyes. He clears his throat before continuing, 'And for what? So that he could claim the ownership of a racehorse. I'm sorry but there is more to it than that, this goes way deeper than any of us realise. Liv you should have at least tried to warn us, if not Emma then you could have got a message to me.'

'You think I don't know that Tom. I feel horrible as it is, you don't need to make it any worse. How was I supposed to know he was going to send someone to wipe her off the road?'

'Guys,' I shout, 'stop.' I wait for them to stop bickering, 'I'm still here. They got to me in time. There's no need to go over what-ifs, should-haves and would-haves.' Despite the steely resolve that comes out of my mouth, I am extremely shaken. My heart rate picks up as all the details sink in. I had always known that Daventhorpe had an extreme chip on his shoulder and a never wrong complex, but I didn't think he was a complete psychopath that would try to kill me to get his own way and cover his tracks. I take a deep breath which is hard considering I have a large incision across my belly that hurt like a bitch.

The nurse comes into the room while we stew in silence. 'Oh hello,' she smiles surprised at the scene she has walked into. 'I've come to check your blood pressure dear and I'm afraid to say that visiting hours are over so anyone other than family must sadly go.' She looks over at Liv as she speaks.

I open my arms the best I can and gesture for her to give me a hug. She looks hesitant to come near me in my battered and bruised condition, but she leans in gently and I feel her warm breath touch my ear. 'You're not to blame.' I whisper into her ear, 'I mean that.'

She pulls back but can't meet my eyes, guilt marring her usually flawless face. She offers a timid wave to Tom and me as she leaves the room. I feel extremely sorry for her even though I am the one that has been injured. I love my best friend, she is more like the sister I never had, and I hate to see her so dejected and forlorn. If I could get up and run around the hospital ward to make her feel better, I would have; unfortunately, I am completely bedridden for the foreseeable future and after that, I fear I will be on crutches for some time.

The nurse wraps the blood pressure cuff around my right arm, prompting Tom to vacate his position perched on the edge of the bed. I wince a little as it tightens harshly around my bicep until it beeps and starts to deflate. I look up trying to read the nurse's expression, but she remains blank. 'Um, your pressure is a little low. Can I see your surgery site?' I nod in reply.

She pulls back the duvet and lifts my hospital gown to one side. 'It is a little swollen so I think it would be best if the surgeon re-examined you.' I feel a lurch of panic. I hate being ill, I hate needles and the thought of surgery spikes fear within me. It was probably a blessing in disguise that I was unconscious through the worst of it. 'Don't worry dear it's just a precaution.' The nurse spies the panicked look on my face. I look up for Tom who stands with his arms crossed, eyes hard focused on my stomach and jaw set in a harsh line once again. He must feel me watching him.

He pulls the chair closer to the bed and sits near to me, holding my hand. 'It'll be ok.' He soothes attempting to alleviate the fear that settles over both of us.

We wait for what seems like a week for the surgeon to come but eventually, he arrives. A tall South African man with sandy-coloured hair examines my abdomen. 'There is more swelling than I would like here.' He pokes and prods a little more and I try not to flinch in pain. 'I think it would be best if you went down for another CT on your abdomen and your head just to be safe.'

'Wait, why my head? I thought you were just worried about my liver and spleen.'

He fixes me with a heavy stare. 'Initially, my primary concern was the internal bleed in your abdomen that is correct, but we were also extremely concerned about a bleed on the brain. Thankfully the primary CT scans came back negative but the drop in your blood pressure is worrying. I don't want to draw any conclusions at this stage. Sometimes these things can come on very slowly, so I think we need to be on the safe side considering you've already come this far. The nurse will take you down as soon as possible.'

'Thank you, doctor.' Tom speaks for me. I try to concentrate on his explanations, but they scare me too much. Brain bleeds are not good. At all. I might need more surgery, I might have a stroke, I might di... I stop my mind from falling off too many cliffs of despair as Tom squeezes my hand a little tighter in both of his.

...

'Hey.' Tom speaks gently standing next to me as I lie outside the CT chamber. 'I'm here.'

'Tom, I'm scared.'

'I know.'

'What if...' I can't finish my sentence my throat is thick with emotion.

'What if what?' he asks tenderly.

'What if I can never ride again? What if I never walk again? What if I'm like this forever?' He silences me with a heart-stopping, fierce, protective kiss. At that moment, my worries fall away and my heart beats only for him.

'That's not going to happen.' He responds as he pulls away, 'Not as long as I walk God's green earth.'

'Wait for me?' I ask as I hear the nurse shuffling towards us in the corridor.

'I'll be here.'

'Forever and always?'

'Forever and always.'

...

As he promised, Tom is waiting for me when I come out of the CT suite. He walks with me as I am wheeled back to my room. We wait in pensive silence for the radiologist to send the results to the doctor so that he can interpret them. Tom reads a magazine while I stare up at the ceiling, unable to concentrate on anything other than what the results could mean.

'Tom?'

'Yeah.'

'Wasn't the entry meant to be done this week for the Racing Post Trophy next month?'

'Don't worry, I got Liv to enter him.'

'But what about Daventhorpe?'

'What about him?' he shrugs. 'After this, he's going to be locked up for a long time.'

'I hope you're right.' A shiver runs down my spine as I ponder the danger he poses to my little family and me.

'But who's been riding him if you've been here the whole time?'

'I rang my sister Phoebe. She's come over and is keeping the horses fit for now. I hope you don't mind.' He looks a little nervous as to what my reaction will be.

'Of course I don't mind. I'm glad I can finally meet her, although I wish it was under better circumstances.' I smile

'The only downside is I think she's corrupted poor little Sam who has been sleeping on her bed in the cottage.' He chuckles

'Oh, bless him. I miss him so much. I just want to get out of here.' I huff

A tap tap tap on the door ends our conversation, my heart jumps in anticipation expecting the doctor to enter the room but instead a nurse comes in holding a bunch of pink peonies and a white cake box.

'These just arrived for you.' The young nurse informs me

as she passes them over. I bring the flowers to my nose and inhale the sweet scent and then pull the card off the plastic.

My Darling Emma

Get well soon!

With all my love,

Clare

Xxx

I smile as I read her card and warmth fills my chest. Clare is the loveliest person and I can't wait to get out of this hospital to give her a big, warm bear hug. I pass the bouquet and card to Tom, then inspect the white cake box. I open the lid and inhale a sharp breath. Inside is a small chocolate fudge cake decorated with one single strawberry. Viola's signature.

'What is it?' asks Tom, concerned.

'Look at this.' I pass him the box. 'Only Viola makes her cakes like this. She must be in the hospital somewhere. Please, Tom, see if you can find her.' I plead.

'But what if the surgeon comes back while I'm gone?

'Please Tom.' I ask again pleading, this time with my eyes. He sprints out of the room in a bid to catch up with her, if she was here at all, leaving the double doors swinging in his wake.

I have so many questions for her. How had she known I was in the hospital? How did she know I needed blood? But most importantly, how did she have the same blood group as me? Were we related? Left only with my internal inquiries for company, I wait yet again for more answers. Attempting to fill the silence of the hospital room, I start to hum to myself. It sounds awful even by my own admission, but it passes the time and helps me concentrate on anything but the CT results and the quandary that surrounded the appearance of Viola.

'You're so weird.' Tom pants as he re-enters the room bending over with his hands on his knees.

'Did you find her?' I question eagerly. I desperately want to speak to our former housekeeper.

'Sorry Em, she is nowhere to be seen. I asked at the nurse's station, at reception and I ran around the car park but it's like she disappeared into thin air.' He informs me as he slumps down in the bedside chair, still breathing heavily.

'Thanks for trying but Tom?'

'Yeah?'

'You'd tell me if you knew anything wouldn't you.' I ask, looking him directly in the eyes. I know he wants to protect me, but I need to know if she is hiding something big from me. She had to be hiding something, she practically bolted from the funeral as soon as Daventhorpe's name came up and I never understood why she left us so many years ago especially when dad needed her, when mum left, quite apart from the fact that she saved my life.

'Em I'm as in the dark in all this as you. When they were giving you the transfusion, they shut me out and wouldn't tell me anything. They just said that you needed blood and

I couldn't be your donor because of your rare group. It was the scariest few hours of my life, they were trying to save you and I couldn't do anything to help. I only found out Viola was the donor because I may have corrupted one of the nurses.'

'What did you do?' I ask warily.

'I may have promised her free tickets to the races for a year.'

'Tom!' I exclaim

'Well, it's lucky she's a big racing fan.' He chuckles, a red blush filling his cheeks. I join him in his laughter, I am in love with the craziest, funniest, most beautiful person I could ever have wished for. He has been my rock through this hell and whatever we have to face in the future, I know he will always be there for me no matter what.

Our laughter is interrupted by the surgeon who enters the room once again, a clipboard in his arms and a stethoscope around his neck. We quickly sober up and Tom shuffles the chair closer, holding my hand tightly in his. The tall, thoughtful man offers me a small smile and I brace myself for the worst. I know what is coming. I know it is going to be bad news. It just is, isn't it?

'Good news Miss Williams, your scan has come back negative. I'm sorry it's taken all day to give you the results. No brain bleed and your liver and spleen, although inflamed, are healing well.'

That is the best news I've heard in forever. 'Thank you so much,' I beam, 'for everything.'

'You're very welcome,' he nods, 'we'll continue to monitor your blood pressure and if it stabilises, we will think about letting you go home.' He gives me a wider smile this time. I turn to Tom and beam widely at him. He grips my hand smiling as wide as me if not wider.

'Thank you, sir.' He stands and shakes the doctor's hand firmly. As he leaves, Tom turns and I squeal in delight jiggling around in the bed, my attempt at a victory dance. He leans over and kisses me. 'Thank God.' He grins, his eyes crinkling at the corners, 'I'm not going to lie, I was shitting myself.' he adds still leant over me.

'You're meant to be the strong one.' I reply beaming from ear to ear. Talk about a weight lifting off my shoulders. Hallelujah!

'You're the strong one, trust me.'

Another knock on the door interrupts our conversation. 'What now?' Tom groans, standing up straight.

'Excuse me miss but there's an officer here to speak with you.'

'Ok send him in.' I reply.

A few seconds later a middle-aged man with dark brown hair and built like a rugby player enters. My hospital room is beginning to feel more like a conveyor belt than a place for rest and recuperation.

'Hello Miss Williams, Mr Doyle, I am Sergeant Robertson from North Yorkshire Police. May I come in?'

'Please.' I gesture to a plastic chair in the corner which he pulls up to the bed.

'Firstly, I must apologise for the circumstances that lead to my visit, but I need to ask you a few questions.' He replies, taking out a small notepad and pen. 'So far we have established that it was a hit and run and unfortunately our primary inquiries would suggest that it was indeed a targeted incident but for now I would like to hear your version of events.'

'Um so…' I look to Tom for support. *You can do this,* he nods. I take a deep breath and continue. 'So, I was driving back from the Winning Post and was about to pull out onto the top road back to the yard when a car came out of nowhere and hit me. He didn't have his lights on or anything I think he must have been waiting for me.' I scrunch my face and shake away the thoughts of that night, unable to handle the fear that diffuses into my head whenever I recollect the crash. 'But I know who was responsible.' I add.

'Well we have linked the car back to a Michael Smith but so far he has alluded capture. He was not present at the scene when the emergency services arrived.' The officer replies. My mouth goes dry at the realisation that Smithy is still out there somewhere.

'Yes, Smithy.' I interject. 'When I was trapped in the car, I could smell him, and I could see lights shining at me, but we know that he was instructed to hit me by Lord Daventhorpe.'

'You believe Lord Daventhorpe is behind this?' he raises

a questioning eyebrow.

'One hundred per cent. He threatened my best friend Liv Matthews at her law firm in Wharton saying that if she began court proceedings against him for the horses he agreed to give to my dad, she'd be sorry and if she told me, she would not get home that night.'

'And you have proof of this?' He queries unconvinced.

'You can talk to Liv she'll tell you.' I urge.

'Thank you, Miss Williams. I will look into this but at this stage, unfortunately, it sounds very much like it is your word against his. I hope you are feeling better soon; we will be in touch.' He shuts his notebook with a clap and stands. 'Here's my card. I'll let myself out.' he nods, handing me his contact details then leaves.

'Well, he was more than useless.' Tom stands and starts to pace, obviously bothered by the officer's lack of interest in Daventhorpe's part in the accident. However, he is right; we do need proof.

'Tom, I'm sure he's trying his best. We of all people know how good he is at covering his tracks.'

'You're too trusting. That's your problem.' He shakes his head.

'Oh, and what now, you think he's corrupting the police now as well.'

'I wouldn't put it past him,' he laughs humourlessly.

'Stop stressing and kiss me.' I say with pleading eyes attempting to halt his patrol of the room. He suspends his assault of the vinyl floor, leans over, his lips find mine and he kisses me.

Chapter Seventeen

Three days later, the doctors are happy to let me go home with the proviso that I rest and come straight back to the hospital if I have any acute abdominal pain, headaches, swelling, feel dizzy or faint.

'No, let your hands carry the weight, relax your shoulders,' the physiotherapist instructs me as I attempt to master my crutches. Having a broken leg sucks. Big time. I could deal with all the other injuries, but my leg stopped me from getting around and that frustrated me. 'Look forward, not down,' she instructs. Tom sniggers in the corner.

'I'm glad you're finding this amusing.' I glare at him to which he puts both hands up in surrender.

'I'll bring the truck around,' he announces, taking my bags with him. I practice with the crutches a little longer and take instructions on how to use them correctly before the physio is happy that I'm not going to fall flat on my face as soon as I am left unsupervised. I perch on the edge of the bed, waiting for Tom to return and ponder the last week's ordeal. The last few months have been a complete roller-coaster, from the withdrawal of the horses to losing dad, meeting Tom, almost dying in a car wreck and training a horse of Flash's stature, my life seems more like a soap opera than the usual day to day monotony I settled upon after dad had got sick.

'Ready?' Tom smiles. He is literally bouncing with delight. I think during the aftermath of the crash, he had thought more than once that this day would never come. Plus, his sister is waiting for us when we got home, and he is so excited to see her. Phoebe has been staying at the yard instead of coming to visit us in the hospital for fear that if left alone, the yard will be vulnerable to an attack from one of Daventhorpe's men. Liv has come to visit most days and can't stop apologising. She has spoken to the police but, as I expected, they are finding it hard to pin the crime to Daventhorpe. Smithy remains on the loose so, like Tom said, the police are being about as good as useless.

'I think so,' I reply.

'Come on then peg-leg.' He jokes referring to the sizeable cast on my right leg.

'I have a pair of crutches and I'm not afraid to use them.'

'Wouldn't expect anything else.' He grins a wide toothy grin at me in reply as he holds open the door for me to hop through. As we venture down the long, straight corridors of the hospital, he places a supportive hand on my back and I hop as quickly as I can. After the second of what seems like never-ending stretches of walkway, I stop for breath, leaning on both crutches, my arms burning from the effort.

'Do you want me to carry you?' Tom asks eyes filled with concern, 'I know you want to be independent after being in bed for over a week but…'

'Yes.'

He looks a little surprised at my reply probably expecting more of a battle, but this is the furthest I have moved in over a week and all the fight has left my broken body. He takes my left crutch first leaning it against the wall before placing his arms under my knees and around my shoulders lifting me into him. He holds the crutches in his right hand at the same time as he carries me to save having to navigate this hospital one more time. I place my head in the crook of his neck and revel in his warmth. I am safe in the arms of the man I love.

When we reach his old truck, he puts me gently back on my feet but supports my weight with his left arm while he opens the truck door before picking me back up and placing me in the seat. He chucks the crutches in the back with a clank while I fasten my seat belt. Tom fires up the engine as I lean back, my eyelids becoming heavy.

…

'Em, hey.' Tom coaxes me out of my sleepy haze. 'We're home.' I open my eyes to the familiar surroundings of the yard. 'Wait there while I get your crutches.' He jumps out and comes around to the passenger side, lifting me onto my feet. I grip his shoulders to steady myself still feeling a little woozy. One by one he hands me my crutches, flings my bag over his shoulder and places a supporting hand on the small of my back as I begin to hop around the corner to the trainer's house. Before I can make it much further, Sam bolts around to meet us, wagging his tail and wiggling his pudgy little body uncontrollably unable to contain his excitement to see us again.

'Hey buddy.' I greet him trying to reach down far enough to stroke him while still balancing on my crutches. Tom seeing my struggle, drops the bag and picks up the batty pug. He licks my face hysterically as a smile tugs at his droopy lips, seeing him immediately bucks up my mood. I would have snuck him into the hospital if I could have. I look up and away from his soggy assault to find a pretty brunette waiting for us in the doorway.

Tom must spot her at the same time as he immediately puts Sam back on the floor and they run over to greet each other. 'Phee,' he calls affectionately and they wrap each other in a tight bear hug. Their resemblance was uncanny, she was the female version of Tom with the same ocean blue eyes, sharp bone structure and slightly wavy brown hair.

'Are you sure you're not a twin?' I ask Tom quizzically as they pull apart, 'You must be Phoebe.' I turn to her, offering a one-arm hug while balancing on one crutch.

'You must be Emma.' She replies holding me so tight that I wobble slightly, 'I've heard so much about you.' she beams

'All good, I hope.' I look across at Tom.

'Oh, very much, he's quite besotted, I've never known him so soppy.' She laughs and nods her head emphatically.

'Thanks for that Phee,' he gives her a pointed look, 'shall we all go inside.' He gestures towards the open door of the house. I hobble into the kitchen with Sam following closely at my heels. Tom pulls a chair out for me at the table which I plop my broken body onto while handing him my crutches. As soon as I am seated Sam hops onto my lap. I wrap myself around him and place a kiss on the top of his head. Phoebe sits across from me while Tom makes us all some tea.

'So, how have the horses been going?' I ask her.

'Really well. Flash is fresh as hell,' she chuckles, 'but he feels amazing. He's everything Tom says he is.'

'How long have we got before the Racing Post Trophy?' I ask Tom, out of kilter from the time I spent unconscious.

'Just over a week.' He replies from across the kitchen.

'What about Silver Noble,' I ask her, 'I thought he was nearly ready to run when I last rode him.'

'Yes, he's been going well. I thought maybe he was a little stiff to pull out yesterday though, so maybe we should all look at him together.'

We go through the remainder of the horses and she gives me her thoughts on each of them individually. 'You sure you don't want a job.' I quip afterwards.

'Don't tempt me,' she laughs, 'I've been offered a job in a big yard back in Ireland and I start in a couple of weeks and besides,' she whispers so Tom can't hear, 'Tom doesn't want me to become caught up with Lord Daventhorpe even though I don't see why I would be.'

'Unfortunately,' I reply glumly, 'he's right.'

We make small talk a little longer and eventually decide to

order in a Chinese takeaway as none of us can be bothered or are in a fit state to cook. After dinner, I bid Phoebe goodnight before she goes back to the yard cottage across from the house. Out of habit and attempting to get back in the real world, I flip open my laptop, hoping to get up to date with some emails. As soon as I load up my inbox, I immediately regret my decision. Ignorance really is bliss. My most recent email is from a certain Mr Lawrence Kent.

Subject: Priory Castle funds
Miss Williams,

Firstly, may I offer my sincere sympathies after hearing of your accident. I do hope you are healing well.

However, I must remind you that the estate of the late Richard Williams still owes my client £250,000. As per the gentleman's agreement between yourself and my client, we are willing to discount the debt owed if the ownership of the horse, Flashdance, is handed over to Lord Daventhorpe.

I hereby give you ten working days to either transfer the funds or transport the horse to Priory Castle at your earliest convenience.
Yours Sincerely,
Lawrence Kent
Kent, Cliff and Dapper Solicitors.

'Is this a joke?' I screech, causing Tom to come running over. 'He only tried to kill me, but that didn't work, so he's just going to file a lawsuit and kill my business instead.' As Tom reads the email over my shoulder, he remains silent but as he continues, I feel him getting tenser and tenser as the anger boils up inside him. 'Tom, say something,' I urge, panic running through my veins. I thought this had been an empty threat, just a veiled attempt to blindside me into turning Flash over to him or his twisted way of getting revenge for the fact that we had kept him. Unfortunately, I have been naïve yet again and I am paying for it now. Daventhorpe will stop at nothing, but I am confused as to why. Surely, he isn't so psychotic that he is prepared to go to such lengths just for a racehorse that may or may not win a race or two. There has to be more to it; I have wracked my brain, again and again, trying to work out what it is but have come up short every time.

'I'm going to do night checks. I need a walk.' Tom informs me, 'Do you want to come?'

'Why aren't you saying anything about this?' I reply, confused.

'Because after the last week you don't want to hear what I think about Daventhorpe. Do you want to come out or not?'

'I'd love to but I don't think I've got the energy,' I shrug, 'and I need to ring Liv to figure out our next move.' I yawn, exhausted.

'Do you want me to help you upstairs?' He asks as he places a kiss on top of my head helping me momentarily to forget the dire situation we are both in.

'No, I think I'll just hobble into the living room for now.' Having been in bed for over a week, I don't want to get straight back in it, not just yet anyway. Plus, I am way too wound up to try to sleep yet.

Before making my way out of the kitchen I ring Liv, she answers almost immediately, 'Em, hey are you home?'

'Yes, we got back this afternoon but Liv, we have a problem.'

'What now?' She asks resigned.

'I'll forward you the email but the top and bottom of it is that we have ten days to find 250K or give Flash to Daventhorpe.'

'What?' She yells down the phone, 'You have got to be joking, that's craziness. Right, don't panic.'

'I'm not the one panicking.' I reply.

'We're going to have to use that list, consequences be dammed.'

'I agree but we need to do it carefully. I'll sleep on it tonight and we can work out the details tomorrow.' I say trying to be pragmatic but underneath I am panicking more than her. We discuss the case at hand a little longer and agree to work out a plan in the morning.

I tuck my phone into my pocket before shuffling myself down the corridor and awkwardly lower myself onto the squishy, brown leather couch. I switch on the TV selecting a random cooking programme, trying my best to focus on the narrator's nasally voice. Tom comes in a little while later and sinks down into the other end of the couch.

'Everything all right? I ask.

'Yes, all good but Phoebe was right, Silver Noble has got a bit of heat in his off-fore knee.' He replies although his main focus is on the woman frying some sort of chicken dish in a wok while giving the camera wide eyes and a knowing smile. Already bored by her attempts at innuendo and euphemism while frying chicken, my mind wanders back over the last few months, everything that has happened and what I am going to do about my new ten-day deadline. I have nearly lost it all, my family, the horses, my life and the sad fact is I still might. Lord Daventhorpe will obviously stop at nothing, but the burning question is why.

I cast my mind back to the last time I was with my dad, a sharp twinge jabs my heart as it pounds in my chest. Even though he was usually asleep or mute when I visited him, I miss him so much. He was the last blood relative I had in this country. You only get one father; I wish I'd never taken him for granted. However, the day Flash won at Thirsk was one of the best days of my life despite Daventhorpe's best efforts to ruin it. I smile to myself, remembering how happy Dad had been.

'Did you see Flash Daddy? Wasn't he amazing?' He nods enthusiastically, smiling on at his trainer and jockey. 'He's gonna be a group 'orse isn't he.'

'P... Pri...' he stammers 'ry... y... ou... n... eed.'

'What's he saying?' Tom whispers in my ear as Dad and

I stare deep into one another's eyes. I try to find clues into what he's saying, it is like he wants to tell me something important but can't find the words.

'Priory?' I question and he nods.

'The castle?' adds Tom and Dad nods again.

Disappointment fills my belly on the realisation that we never found anything particularly concrete during our trip to Priory Castle. Although, how dad knew Lord Daventhorpe would threaten us with a scandal involving Priory Castle worried me. Could he really have taken a backhander of 250K? I shake away the thought unconvinced that it is possible. Instead, I study the many winner's photos that adorn the living room walls. I look across at the picture of the beautiful grey filly Lady Daventhorpe winning the Oaks with Robbie. Oh Robbie, stupid Robbie, he hasn't even texted to see if I am ok but then again, he is probably in on the whole thing. Next to that is the largest picture in the room, the now infamous Priory Castle winning the King George Stakes at Glorious Goodwood. He was a stocky chestnut colt with a white star, flaxen mane and tail, and I remember that he would only ever let one specific lad in the stable with him. He could be a savage, but he was incredibly fast and that was all that mattered. Priory Castle was seriously impressive that day, he beat some of the best sprinters in Europe and made the rest of the field look slow. Dad was so happy, he had been readying him for that race all season. The large gold framed photograph is positioned higher than the others and is set in a deep oak frame which somehow makes the photo seem as if it is bigger and pushed further forward. I glance over to the next photo but then it hits me. Maybe I've been wrong this entire time. Maybe dad was talking about the horse, not the place.

'Tom.' I half-shout, causing him to jump out of his TV trance, 'It's the photo.'

'What photo?' he asks, confused looking around the room.

'Priory Castle. The photo. It must be the photo.' I can't get the words out fast enough.

'Slow down Em. I literally have no idea what you're talking about.'

'Ok,' I let out a long breath trying to steady my racing heart, 'when we went to see dad, he said you need Priory Castle right?'

'Right?'

'Maybe he didn't mean the place, maybe he meant the horse. In the photo!' I point, 'Tom I'm telling you there's something in that photo.' He continues to give me a quizzical look, 'Oh don't bother I'll look.' I begin a futile attempt to lift myself off the couch and over to the photo, but Tom pulls me back down.

'Stop you crazy woman, let me do it.' He gets to his feet, hoists the picture off the wall and lays it face down on the coffee table. The back is slightly peeling in the bottom right-hand corner.

'Pull it,' I instruct.

'Are you sure about this?' He replies, reluctant to damage the backing.

'Yes!'

'Well, ok then.' He carefully peels back the black paper, doing his best to prevent it from ripping. I look on like a kid at Christmas hoping that the present wrapped inside is what you wished for. I want to scream and shout at him to just rip it all off, but I bite my tongue and pray and pray that there is something inside and I'm not high on pain killers. As he continues to pull off the back, some papers come into view, he stops, looks up and a wide smile spreads over his lips.

'Keep going.' I urge desperate to see what really lies inside.

Suddenly with one final flourish, he tears off the back and a pile of neatly stacked papers are revealed.

'Sweet Jesus.' Tom picks up the top sheet and his eyes widen as he deciphers the page. Without warning, he grips my cheeks with both hands and steals my breath with a heart-stopping kiss.

'What the...?' I ask bewildered as I watch him beam enthusiastically at me.

'Look at this.' He passes me the first sheet. I hesitantly take the document scanning the page, my heart beating wildly as I do.

'Lord above, Daventhorpe has been backing his own horses to lose!' I exclaim, no wonder he's got so much money, he was winning over half a million a week.'

'I guess it would explain why he's also run out of money as he was losing hundreds of thousands too. This next sheet says he lost nearly one million.' Tom adds scanning over the second sheet of betting receipts.

'So that's why he's been hounding me for cash. He's run out of money although by the looks of things 250K isn't going to get anywhere near it.'

'But why Flash?' Asks Tom looking up.

'Flash is his get out of jail card, I guess. He would have either sold him to pay off his debts or tried to win a shed load of prize money. He must have known someone was onto him so he stopped laying his own horses. It also explains why Robbie had so much loose cash. He was obviously the one doing the stopping, but what if dad was in on it too? Why did dad have all Lord Daventhorpe's betting records hidden behind a picture? Could he have been involved in a betting scam with that hateful man? The thought was mindblowing.

'I tell you what, I'm literally speechless.' I stammer, finishing my assessments, but Tom is miles away perusing another piece of the paper trail dad left us.

'Em,' he speaks, 'I think you need to see this.' His eyes speak a thousand words and I brace myself for whatever it is he has found. I take the paper from him and inhale sharply as I recognise the familiar swirly handwriting.

Dearest Emma,

If you're reading this I am probably ill, dead or Daventhorpe's locked me up, but you should know that wherever I am, I am so proud of you and the wonderful person you have become.

I know that I was not always the most hands-on father to you, but you should know that everything I ever did and everything I ever achieved was always and only for you.

The documents you have so cleverly found are extremely important darling girl, and as soon as you read this, you must call the police. Silus Daventhorpe is a very dangerous man and was trying to ruin me as a trainer by getting me to stop his horses but I refused much to his disgust. Instead, he employed his very own 'stopping jockey' Robert James who did his dirty work for him against my will. I hope that by finding these documents, it will enable you to be free of him. I am truly sorry that I never did this myself and set you free from him sooner, but he held something over me that I could never undo. Please believe me when I tell you I was never involved in any of this, and whatever he will undoubtedly say I never took a penny from him.

Please know that I will always love you and so will my darling Viola. All I ask is that you love generously, forgive freely and regret nothing.

Love forever and always,

Dad X

I finish reading his letter and wipe away an errant tear that runs down my cheek. I can hear him in every word, feeling his absence more abundantly than ever. I think back to the last few years that dad was training and the constant phone calls from Lord Daventhorpe, which always ended up with my dad slamming the phone down and angrily stomping upstairs to his room. An atmosphere would hang heavily in the house and I used to escape by riding Gremlin over the moors for hours just to get away from it.

Tom comes to sit beside me, wrapping an arm around my shoulder. Sometimes in life one moment can change the course of your whole existence, whether that is the moment you fall in love, the day you finally win that race, or the moment you discover the one thing you've been looking for that causes everything to fall into place and fit together. This was our life-changing moment. One day we would look back and remember the night we finally had the power to set ourselves free from the one person that had held us captive for so long.

'Oh, gees,' I shiver, 'he always did have a way with words. Tom?'

'Mmmhmm.'

'What about Viola? There's something I do not see here. Do you think she's more than I thought she was, I mean she must be?'

'Do you?' He replies.

'Maybe. I guess. I don't know.' I ramble, confusion

clouding my every thought. 'What now?' I ask, looking into his eyes.

'It's time to be free from him and start living.'

Chapter Eighteen

Two days later Tom, Liv, Sergeant Robertson and I sit around the kitchen table accompanied by Superintendent David Lloyd-Jones and Chief Superintendent Gordon Richards of the Metropolitan Police. I had called Sergeant Robertson the night we had found the betting documents but due to the sheer amount of money that was being gambled to lose, he, alongside the BHA, had no choice but to bring in the London officers. I had handed over all the documents enclosed behind the photo which they placed in sealed plastic evidence bags.

'So, what now?' I question the London officers. My question is interrupted by the shrill ringing of a phone.

The Chief Superintendent shuffles in his seat and pulls out his mobile. 'Sorry I must take this.' He announces before letting himself briefly out of the kitchen. I strain my ears trying to listen to his conversation, but it is very short and before I catch anything that is said, he comes back in.

'Good news.' He informs us as he retakes his seat, 'Lord Daventhorpe has just been taken into custody by one of my colleagues.'

I look across to Liv and Tom; we all share an emphatic but relieved smile.

'What happens now? Asks Tom.

'Well, we alongside the BHA will build a case against him and judging by the evidence we already have, that will not be hard. For now, he will remain in custody and we will do our best to keep him there.'

'Can I be honest with you?' I interject

'Yes please?' He offers

'I am concerned that he will come after me and after the crash, I'm worried how far he might go to get revenge, especially with Smithy still on the loose.'

'I completely understand your concerns. Aside from the clear breaches of the rules of racing, we also have an ongoing inquiry of fraud, blackmail and tax evasion. At the present time, Mr Smith is still at large, but I am assured by Sergeant Robertson that he has just assigned more officers in pursuit of his capture.'

'And what about the other letter and the list of horses that were promised to my dad. Do we have any claim over them or not?'

For now, it is hard to say but you and your late father are owed a lot of money and potentially compensation as a result of the crash; therefore, you may find yourself with many horses in place of the funds owed. For now, however, sit tight and let it play out.'

As he finishes his sentence, his deputy leans across and whispers something in his ear to which he nods. 'We must be going but please call me on my direct line if you have any concerns.'

'Thank you.' I shake his and his deputy's hand as they rise from the table, Tom does the same as we bid farewell to the trio of officers.

'Hey guys is it safe to come in now?' Calls Phoebe from the doorway.

'Yes, Phee come in.' Replies Tom.

'Group hug.' Liv calls as Phoebe enters. We wrap our arms tightly around each other, our heads coming together as we form a circle.

'We did it guys. I just want to say I love you all. You're my family and I don't know what I would have done without you.'

'I don't know whether to cry, pray or open some champagne.' Adds Liv mirroring my own smile and visibly holding back tears.

As we break apart, Tom runs a hand down his face and then pulls me into him and kisses the top of my head. 'I don't think I've ever felt so vindicated as I do at this moment.' He speaks into my hair. I hug him tighter, breathing him in and listening to his beating heart. We've done it, we've ended his hold over us and from this moment on we will not be beholden to anyone ever again. Not ever.

'Now all the heavies have gone, can we start riding out?' Asks Phoebe interrupting our hugging session.

'Yes!' I exclaim, 'Please give me some normality.'

'I place dibs on Flash.' She smiles sweetly at me.

'Sorry Phee not happening.' Tom swats her arms with the back of his hand as he clears away the used coffee cups from the table. She juts out her bottom lip as if to throw a tantrum.

'Sorry, he's right. It will be his last piece of work before the Racing Post on Saturday. I need you to ride Divine Right upsides him though.'

'Ok, I'll forgive you.' She replies.

…

For the first time ever, I stand at the top of the gallops feeling genuinely happy now that I no longer have Daventhorpe's heavy cloud hanging over me. From now on, we can live how we want. We can go about our lives without fear of the consequences and most importantly, we can look forward to a future filled with happiness and love, without sadness and regrets. However, one final question looms over me, where and who is Viola? Had I known her at all and why did dad refer to her as *my darling Viola*?

The thunder of hoofbeats rocks me out of my thoughts. I pull the binoculars up to my face while balancing on a crutch as Tom and Phoebe sprint up the gallop towards me, woodchip flying in their wake. The sun bounces off the horse's coats as they stride past me. Flash looks as good as ever and hope fills my belly at the prospect of finally running him in the Racing Post Trophy without having to worry about the consequences.

I heave myself back into the gallop jeep and Liv drives us both back to the yard. 'That was impressive.' She comments as she carefully negotiates the bumps and ridges of the moor aware that my leg is still in plaster.

'Everything crossed for Saturday.' I reply.

…

It is mid-afternoon by the time the horses have all been exercised and fed. Liv and Phoebe have gone to Wharton to pick up some groceries. Tom flips through the Racing Post while stuffing his face with a ham sandwich and I swirl coffee around my mug searching for I don't know what.

'Tom, do you think I should track down Viola. I need to thank her for saving my life at least.'

He looks up from the paper and meets me with a steady gaze. 'Do you even know where she lives?'

'She used to live in a little cottage near Ripon. It's worth a try, isn't it?'

'Look Em,' he places his mug back on its a coaster, 'I've been a part of many of the decisions through all this, but this is your choice to make. I'll support you whatever you decide.'

'Will you drive me?' I reply as anxiety rises up inside me. I know I have to do this. I have to know why she saved me that day, how she knew, and what the true story is.

'Of course.'

I hobble out to Tom's truck, as I have yet to replace my poor Golf, and clamber in. I am on the mend but unfortunately, it will be another month before I can have my cast off.

Half an hour later, we reach a wooded area on the

outskirts of Ripon.

'Turn left up there,' I direct Tom who flicks on the indicator, 'and then follow the road to the right.' A small, white, ivy-clad cottage comes into view set alone at the end of the clearing.

Tom puts the truck in park just outside the cottage and leans into the back seat to fetch my crutches. 'Do you want me to come in with you?' He asks.

'No, I need to do this by myself.' I reply before opening the door. He comes around to help me out but goes no further giving me the time and space to deal with whatever I am about to face. I hop over to the door knocking gently, waiting to see if Viola will answer. I am overcome with nerves and jitters as I stand on the cottage porch afraid that what I am about to find out will reveal a nest of lies that my life has been built on. When you are a child life is pretty simple, you have a mum, a dad, best friends and you know that you are loved unconditionally, and every day is a happy one. But as you grow up, you so badly want to be an adult and make your own decisions, to stay up late or eat all the chocolate biscuits. However, the reality of it sucks. Suddenly you're left on your own to fend for yourself, you decide the things you wanted as a ten-year-old thinking about the future really don't matter. You would give anything to go back to the time when everything was happy and the biggest drama in your life was who you were going to sit next to at school. Even though for the first time in a very long time, I feel loved and supported, the nagging feeling that my whole life has been built on a lie remains. Who really is Viola? Why was she my dad's darling? And why the hell am I only looking for answers now?

There is no movement in the house that I can see. I try another knock on the door, a little harder this time. Something inside the house causes the thin cotton curtain to shift in the window frame. My heart lurches and I knock again. Suddenly, the door creaks open a slither, enough for a voice to be heard. 'Please, you can't be here,' she begs, closing the door slightly.

Anticipating the movement, I jam my crutch in the door frame, preventing her from closing it. 'Viola,' I call, you don't need to be afraid anymore. I just want to talk. Daventhorpe has been taken into custody, he can't hurt us ever again,' I plead, 'Lola?' I try. I keep my crutch there for a few more seconds before she opens the door wide revealing herself. Her curled greying hair hangs loosely around her shoulders, her petite slender frame mirrors that of my own and her generous green eyes convey the nervous energy I feel in this moment with her. 'Please, can I come in?' I ask gently. She gestures for me to follow her and she leads us into a small sitting-room with deep couches and an intricate, well-used fireplace.

'I'll go make us some tea.' She announces. I twiddle my fingers and peruse the ceiling nervously waiting for her to return. I jump suddenly, probably more than necessary as a result of the nervous energy whirling around my body when a grey, slinky cat hops onto the top of the mantelpiece.

'Oh Morris, do get down!' Scolds Viola who returns carrying a tray of tea. She hands me a steaming hot mug before sitting across from me on a single sofa chair.

I wait a few seconds and take a courteous sip of tea before starting, 'Viola, how did you know I was in the hospital? And why do we have the same blood group?' I get straight to the point; I had waited a long time for answers.

'I'm glad you're on the mend darling girl. Your poor Tommy was beside himself.' She answers, taking another drink of tea.

'Lola, please I need some kind of explanation.'

'Darling girl if only you knew.' She sighs, trying to avoid eye contact. The knots in my stomach turn over and over each other while I take a steadying breath.

'Look I know this is as strange for you as it probably is for me, but you should know that dad left a load of documents incriminating Daventhorpe, so much so that he no longer has a say in our lives. He can't and won't hurt us any longer so please, this is the last piece of the puzzle, I've got to know, are you my mother?' As I say the final word, her eyes widen and fly up to meet my own. It is then that I know my gut was right all along.

'But how did you know?' She whispers at a loss for words and close to tears. I have to take a deep breath of my own. When Tom had told me Viola had been called in to give blood, I wracked my brain and went over and over possible scenarios as to how she could be in the same blood group as me but I kept coming up with the same answer. She had to be a blood relative at least and most scarily of all, she could be the loving mother I never had. She had, after all, practically raised me.

'All I ask of you is that you tell me the truth.' I speak trying to keep a lock on my emotions and retain a tight grip on the situation. This isn't easy for either of us but I have to hear the truth.

'Well, I suppose I better start at the beginning.' She replies, trying a smile as she casts her mind back. 'I was your father's housekeeper when he very first starting training over thirty years ago. We got along very well, I kept him company really. I got all his meals for him, cleaned the house, helped him with owners, organised his life. Eventually, we fell in love. We spent a short but very happy time together and we planned to get married when the time was right. However, when Lord Daventhorpe approached Richard to become his private trainer, he had one condition, that he married first. Your father was only too happy to agree, after all, we were together. All we had to do was get a license and walk down the aisle. But as always, Daventhorpe had other ideas, he told Richard that he must marry well, a lowly housekeeper would never do as far as he was concerned. We had no other choice but to split up. I refused to stand between him and his burgeoning career. I felt that if I did, he would resent me for it further down the line.

Anyway, in a very short space of time, Richard married Kathleen. Shortly after, I found out I was pregnant, with you. I went to Richard and told him, he was overjoyed and we were still very much in love. At this point, I was no longer working for him anymore and I was all set to raise you myself as a single mother even though it was frowned upon in those days, but then Kathleen fell pregnant at the same time. However, she miscarried late in her pregnancy and even though your father didn't feel the same for her as he did for me, he was still devastated to lose the baby. So when you were born we made a deal, instead of me raising you singlehandedly with nothing, he and Kathleen would raise you as their own and I would come back as housekeeper so I could watch you grow up. It might sound crazy, but it was my only chance to play a part in your life.'

I am heartbroken as she explains her story to me, but not just for me, for her. I swallow a lump in my throat. I could very easily break down in a fit of unbridled tears but I know I have to be strong for her, after all I can't imagine being prevented from being with Tom based on our social status to then watch him raise our child with another woman. That would be inconceivable torture.

'I'm just so sorry, Emma love.' She sniffles, taking out a cotton hanky. 'We made a pact that you would never find out.' She dabs gently at her eyes.

'But why did you leave to go work for Daventhorpe?' I

ask confused knowing he was the reason that they split up.

'Because he found out that you were my daughter. He blackmailed me into passing him inside information about the horses in exchange for keeping mine and Richard's secret. I wanted to protect you and if working for him was what it took, I was willing to pay that price.'

'So you knew about the gambling?'

'I knew he was doing something illegal, I just had no power to stop it, so I left your father for good but in true Daventhorpe style he made me come and work for him in exchange for never telling you the real truth.' Her head droops ashamed as her tears fall.

'And did you know about the betting slips?' I ask and she nods in reply, so I continue, 'Why did you save them all and how did they end up behind the picture of Priory Castle in our living room?

'I couldn't cope with the lies, scandal and threats. I decided I had to leave. On my last day, I scoured the castle for documents that would either help me leave or most importantly help Richard. It was the only way that I could protect your father from that man. I knew that one day if anything ever happened, it could be traced back to that hideous man and justice might be done.' She can't meet my eyes as she recounts past events.

'If I could get up and walk, I'd give you a hug right now.' I smile. She looks up, surprised at my words. 'Do you want to hear how I see it?' I ask her and she nods in reply.

'I love my dad, I always have, and I always will. I didn't always agree with his decisions and I don't truly understand his reasoning behind taking Daventhorpe's job in exchange for leaving you, but I forgive him and most importantly I forgive you, and I want you to know that I love you and I always have. My mum or Kathleen,' I substitute my words, 'was never kind to me and I lived my whole life thinking that I was the only child in the world that had a mother that didn't love her, but now I've been set free. I've finally found you Viola, and now we can leave all our regrets in the past because the future is for the taking, and I've decided that I'm going to grab mine with both hands. Please tell me you want to be a part of it?'

'Oh darling girl,' she speaks between tears, 'I've never wanted anything more.'

Chapter Nineteen

Tonight, we are having a pre-Racing Post Trophy dinner to celebrate new family, new friends and new beginnings. Clare, her husband Chris, Phoebe, Liv, Tom and most importantly Viola are all sitting around our oversized kitchen table.

'So, who's excited for tomorrow?' Says Liv serving herself a mountain of salad to add to her spaghetti bolognese that Tom and I have managed to throw together at the last minute.

'I'll let you know.' I chuckle, butterflies whirling around my stomach. The last week has been a rollercoaster; that is saying something considering the weeks before that. The London officers notified us that Lord Daventhorpe would remain in custody for the foreseeable future, which is an incredible weight off my mind. However, Smithy still eludes capture. Tom has taken me to see Viola every day and I have offered her one of the yard cottages to live in, but she is yet to give me her answer to that. I am still getting used to the idea that she is really my mother, but Tom has been helping me work through it so that it doesn't mess up my head too much.

As we settle down to eat, I decide to say a few words. 'I'd

just like to thank everyone for coming tonight, it means a lot to me.' I smile. 'I'd also like to introduce you all to Tom's sister Phoebe who I hope you will be seeing more of and also I'd like to introduce my real mum to you all, Viola. To the future.' I raise my glass in a toast.

'To the future.' Everyone replies in unison. Viola looks a little taken aback probably getting used to the new paradigm as much as me, but she looks content at the same time. For dessert, we have nothing other than one of Viola's show-stopping chocolate fudge cakes.

'Wow, Viola, this cake is beyond incredible! I could bathe in it for a week,' exclaims Phoebe licking her fork. Viola smiles across at her but Tom shifts in his seat, 'I hope that's just a figure of speech Phee.'

'Oh, big brother, do be quiet.' She replies, giving him a glare.

'She's right.' Adds Clare, 'This is in a different league to what my chef makes at the Winning Post. I think you need to give him some lessons.'

'You're all too kind,' Viola replies a little embarrassed at their antics focusing on her own plate.

It is past eleven by the time everyone leaves. For the first time in a while, I'm not tired, probably because I'm high on chocolate fudge cake and painkillers. I sit at the table as Tom clears the last of the plates into the dishwasher.

'Do you think they'll ever catch Smithy?' I question, more to myself than to Tom, a slight shiver running down my spine.

'He'd better hope they catch him before I do.' He replies darkly.

'Tom, I'm worried.' A sense of foreboding clouds the happy state that I have enjoyed all through dinner.

'About what?' He asks, closing up the dishwasher.

'I know Daventhorpe is inside now but I'm worried that someone might try to hurt Flash, tomorrow is the biggest day, not just in his career, but for us too. It's not like he ever worked single-handedly before, we know that better than anyone.'

'I know.' He sighs, 'I'm with you on that one.'

'I want to sleep in the barn tonight.'

'You want to sleep in the barn tonight?' He replies.

'Yep. Dad always used to make one of the lads do it before a big race just in case. So tonight, I'm going to. I won't settle unless I know he's safe. This is our time now. I won't let anyone jeopardise that.'

Tom agrees and runs upstairs to fetch some pillows, sleeping bags and warm clothes. When he returns, we make our way into the chilly October air. We wrap up with two jackets each, a fluffy hat and gloves. He pulls the wooden sliding door back to a chorus of snickers and snuffles. I flick on the lights while Tom pulls a couple of shavings bales together in a make-shift bed before laying down the sleeping bags and pillows. I snuggle in, doing my best to get comfy while Tom switches off the lights. He wriggles in behind me, wrapping his arms around me sharing my heat. I turn around and give him a long, tender kiss in the darkness of the barn.

'What was that for?' He chuckles.

'It's because I love you.' I smile into the darkness.

'And I love you Em, I love you.' He replies before we drift off to sleep the horses our only company.

…

'Help.' I try to scream to no avail. The car crumples around me, searing pain radiates through my body. I am helpless, unable to move. Lights are flickering, flashing, brighter, dimmer and that odour I can smell. It permeates all my senses and I cannot escape it. Woof, woof, woof. Woof, woof woof. 'Shut up you little shit.' A strained voice whispers. I jolt awake. My heart races. Where am I? How did I escape the car? My brain suddenly rights itself and I realise that I am in fact in the barn with Tom sleeping soundly next to me. I let out a ragged breath. Why did I keep having nightmares about the crash? Woof, woof, woof. Sam? How had he got out and why is he barking?

'Tom.' I jostle him awake.

'Hmm.' He groans, his voice thick with sleep.

'Wake up.' I urge, 'I think there's someone out there.'

'Huh? What?' He sits up immediately wide awake, untangling himself from the sleeping bag. He passes me my crutches. 'Use these if you have to,' he instructs, no word of a joke in his tone. He marches off into the darkness, leaving me alone with only my crutches to defend me. He is gone for some time scouring the yard for intruders.

My eyes adjust to the darkness focusing on anything that moves. I strain my ears listening to any sound in case someone or something hides in the shadows. Despite the late hour, my body remains on high alert thanks to the adrenaline pumping in my system. I jump as I hear the barn door slide open just a crack. The sounds of footsteps increase as the person gets closer and I start to feel relief wash over me as I hear what I believe to be Tom returning, but it is then that I smell him, the alcohol, the body odour, the rotten cabbages. Smithy.

I sit in deathly silence, not wanting to spook him, knowing that with only one functioning leg, he could easily get away or hurt me more than I could ever hurt him. His heavy boots clump onto the concrete floor despite his best efforts to avoid detection. He gets closer still and I see the light from his torch scanning the horse's names on the stable doors. I wait until he is reaching up to open Flash's door to make a move. I strike him as hard as I can on the knee, a sickening crack ringing out into the darkness, 'What the…' He screams out in pain.

I strike him again, causing him to fall to the ground. Something is thrown from his hand and clatters onto the concrete floor of the barn, some distance away. He grabs at my neck with his rough, calloused hands pulling me down with him, then he presses into the sensitive cartilage in my throat and I wretch. As he lifts his fingers to press down again, I scream at the top of my lungs, anything to get Tom to hear me. 'Tom!' I scream again, Tom, in here!'

He shoves his knee into my stomach to keep me down. I yelp in pain, the area still sore from the surgery. My brain flicks between the crash and the present moment and I feel numb, unable to move, my body is close to useless. For what seems like an eternity, I am paralysed. All I can feel is Smithy's weight bearing down on me, his disgusting breath in my face and all I think of is that I am going to die. Then with one mighty effort, I force myself to react and reach into the present moment searching for that inner fire I know I have inside me. With him jabbing me onto the cold concrete floor my only weapon is my mouth and I bite the tender skin of his arm with as much force as my jaw can render. In the darkness, I see the white of his eyes light up as he realises what I have done to him. He raises his right arm high above his head, his fist curling into a tight ball. I squish my eyes closed ready to receive the impending blow, but it never comes. Suddenly, the unwelcome warmth of his heavy body is wrenched from above me as Tom grabs him by his collar and fires him onto the concrete floor beside me.

'Call the police.' Tom yells. I gather myself as quickly as possible shuffling back to the bales on my bottom feeling around for my phone as I do while Tom pins Smithy to the ground. Another rush of adrenaline fires into me as I lay my hands on the phone, the screen lights up. I dial the emergency number as fast as my fingers can physically move. I hold it up to my ear willing the line to connect, after a few rings the line clicks in and I quickly rattle off the situation without pausing for breath. The receiver assures me that an officer will be with us in the next ten minutes but stays on the line in case of any further emergency.

'How long?' Tom grates using all his strength to hold a raging Smithy to the floor.

'Ten minutes.' I reply

'Maybe I should have wiped you out as well Doyle.' Smithy mumbles in his characteristic drawl.

'Shut up.' Tom pushes him harder into the floor at which he laughs sadistically before he is silent once again. Time slows to a glacial pace as we wait for the police, where seconds feel like hours and minutes feel like days. Tom manages to hold Smithy down, bending both arms behind his back. He looks weary from having to keep such a tight grip on him although it seems Smithy has relaxed, accepting his fate. At long last, the sound of shrill, high-pitched sirens ring loud into the quiet night. Glowing blue lights illuminate the darkness and advance into the yard. I look down at Smithy as the police quickly disembark from their vehicles, his body is limp and his face blank but without warning, he makes one last attempt to evade capture. As Tom switches his attention to the advancing police officers, Smithy uses the distraction to bring his head back to butt Tom hard in the chest. Tom cries out in pain as Smithy pulls himself up to stand and is legging it down the barn before anyone can react. The horses kick and rear in their stalls startled by the sudden turn of events.

'Tom!' I cry, awkwardly dropping down next to him.

Police officers race past us sprinting after Smithy, their heavy boots clumping as they go, their radios blasting out calling for back up. Tom takes a steadying breath, visibly winded by the unexpected blow to his chest.

A vociferous crack sounds from the other end of the barn causing all occupants, horse and human to jump with fright. Next, a different officer sprints past us and we all turn our attention to him following his urgent passage down the barn, the thump of his boots and the crackle of his radio adding to the chaos. I wrap an arm around Tom as he settles his breathing into a steady rhythm.

'What's going on?' Phoebe, flustered, sprints into the barn dressed in pyjamas and wellies, her eyes widening as she takes in the scene in front of her with Tom on the floor, a makeshift bed and most disconcerting of all a crowd of police officers and sirens at the other end of the barn. I turn to answer her but once again my attention is diverted as two police officers drag an unconscious Smithy back past us accompanied by another officer who leads the way.

'What happened? I query the police officer.

'We had to use the taser. Don't worry miss, it's all under control.' His eyes flick to Tom bent over on the floor. 'Do we need an ambulance?' He asks

'No, no, I'm fine.' Tom replies, his voice a little raspy.

Phoebe squats down on the other side of him her eyes filled with concern. 'What happened Tom?'

'Smithy head-butted him right in the ribs.' I answer for him.

'It's nothing Phee.' He mumbles, 'Help me up, will you?'

Phoebe and I exchange worried glances but take his word for it. She grabs both his hands pulling him to his feet, then does the same to me, handing me my crutches to balance on.

'What's that?' Phoebe screeches, eyes widening as she points to a needle and syringe full of a cloudy liquid on the floor near Flash's stable. My heart lurches in my chest, Smithy must have come here tonight to drug Flash. Even though I suspected he was doing exactly this the harsh reality of seeing the full syringe rocks me to my core, the magnitude of Daventhorpe's influence even as he rots in prison is apparent for all to see.

'Badge 498 come in, we have a situation in the barn.' The officer speaks into the radio.

Another officer arrives and places the syringe in a plastic evidence bag.

'Miss?' The officer addresses me.

'Yes, sorry.' I reply, giving him my full attention.

'Just to let you know that I have an officer doing a final search of the property to make sure that all threats have been eliminated but we will leave an armed officer on the yard tonight for your own protection. We will now take the suspect into custody. Someone will be in touch to let you know the outcome.' He shakes my hand.

'Yes, thank you.' I nod.

'Are you ok?' Tom pulls me into a gentle embrace.

'I'm fine, I'm more worried about you. Are you going to be able to ride tomorrow?'

'I'm fine,' he repeats. I fix him with an I don't believe you stare, 'I am!' He exclaims, 'I promise.' He lowers his voice.

'Flash looks fine.' Phoebe announces closing his stable door after checking him over.

'You guys go in.' I tell them, 'I want a moment alone with him.'

'You sure?' asks Tom.

'I'm sure.'

As they leave, I hop over to his stable and he comes to the front, putting his head over the door.

'Hey you.' I breathe gazing into his deep, brown eyes. 'I love you.' I tell him soppily, a wave of emotion washing over me. 'It's going to be hard tomorrow Flashy. You're going to have to use your whole heart but whatever happens, you've taken me on a journey I could never have imagined so thank you.' He looks right back at me and into my soul as I speak to him and it is then that I am certain, even if he doesn't understand the words, he knows. I kiss him gently on the nose revelling in the velvety softness and his warm breath. I give him a pat on the neck before hopping to the light switch at the end of the barn. I glance back to find he has followed my every step, watching me intently. We share a final knowing look and I switch the lights off.

Chapter Twenty

Doncaster racecourse is alive with anticipation. Excited racegoers swarm around the track straining to catch a glimpse of the horses as they canter down to the start, eager to spot a future champion. Dramatic music blasts out overhead. Various trainers and connections are besieged by the press mob, shoving cameras and microphones in their faces, striving to get the inside line on their runners, building the tension even further. Liv, Phoebe and I stand to one side in the parade ring watching the big screen, waiting apprehensively, left out in the cold by the press who surround John Denson the trainer of the market leader Blast Of Colour. This morning Flashdance was priced at the insultingly big odds of 40-1 although he has now moved into 20-1. It seems no one has taken him seriously, but I still believe. I don't need the affirmation of the bookies and the press. The only talking that matters will be done on the racecourse.

The autumn wind swirls around us and I shiver underneath my thick dress coat. Standing side by side, we take each other's hands squeezing gently, lending each other support in a show of solidarity. We are a team, we are in this together, we are a family. We have waited for this moment for so long.

As I take a steadying breath to calm my racing heart, I think back to everything that has led me to this moment. When dad got sick, my world fell apart, when Daventhorpe pulled all of his horses out of the yard, I thought I had failed him. As I ran from Daventhorpe's depravity, I literally sprinted into the man that would change my life forever, who made me better, who helped me believe and who awakened the fire inside of me that the world had very nearly burnt out. As I stand here, after everything that I have been through, I feel stronger and for the first time, I truly believe. Flash is ready, we are ready, I am ready. *This* is our time now. The commentators' booming voice interrupts my thoughts.

'And they're off! They race away, the straight mile ahead of them for this the Racing Post Trophy. Jorvik breaks smartly in the centre of the course alongside Dunlop with Perfect Dream tracking them in third. Flashdance in the red and blue colours sits midfield with the green cap of Chapter and Verse upsides him. Blast Of Colour the market leader waits patiently in the rear as usual with Painted Cave pushed along to keep up behind him. But it's Jorvik in the maroon colours that leads the charge smartly upfront taking a couple of lengths advantage on the field. Dunlop and Perfect Dream race together in second and third with Flashdance slotted in behind them in fourth. The final five furlongs are now in front of them, with no one willing to make a move but Jorvik and Matthew Harper set an even gallop and are two lengths up on the field. Flashdance pulls strongly in behind causing Tom Doyle to restrain him a little harder than he would like in behind the front runners. Blast Of Colour looks comfortable in behind and Painted Cave sits on his heels. They're already at the three-furlong pole and Jorvik retains his advantage on the field Dunlop gives chase trying to find a way out from his position in midfield. Now young Tom Doyle pulls Flash Dance out of the pack and lets him stride upsides Jorvik, the pair matching strides. They're beginning to lengthen, the final two furlongs in sight.'

The field charge on, the stands looming up ahead inciting a deafening roar from the packed-out crowds who shout their runners home. I watch on in silence, the race unfolding before my eyes unable to breathe, hoping and praying that he can do it.

'Flashdance takes the lead from Jorvik with the favourite Blast Of Colour tracking these two yet to make a move. The race now developing into a sprint as the three front runners race in line, Flashdance the meat in the sandwich as he is urged forward to take the lead and they head into the final furlong. Blast Of Colour goes on by half a length but Flashdance battles back against him and Jorvik can't go with them. And it's Blast of Colour that goes on again but Flashdance is coming back, it's Flashdance and Blast of Colour together as they head for the line. Heads up, heads down, oh it's desperate!'

'Go on Tom!' We scream in unison as they charge past

the post. I drop to my knees as they cross the line together. Has he won it? Were we second, beaten by a whisker? In this moment as the judge calls a photo finish I look to the heavens and pray that today this will go our way, that the stars will align in our favour and the dream will stay alive.

I hop out to the track as fast as I can, adrenaline pumping through my veins, my heart beating wildly. Liv leads Flash and Tom around in a circle on the racecourse as we wait with bated breath for the result. The racecourse is silent. No one knows who has won. The cold, blustery wind swirls around Town Moor as we wait, and we wait, and we wait. I look at Tom, he looks at me. I look to the heavens; the heavens look back.

'The result of the photo finish for first place…' We all stop. and I grip Tom's hand and place another on Flash's mane. 'First, number three, Flashdance.'

'Oh my God! Oh my God!' I scream, jumping up and down on my good leg. Tom hugs Flash around his neck and kisses him. Phoebe barrels into me, wrapping me in a hug crying like a baby. Liv joins her in ecstatic, delirious sobbing. A lone tear escapes down my own cheek and I place a hand over my mouth in a bid to contain the tsunami of emotion that washes over me.

Tom leans down from Flash and whispers, 'We did it.' I smile at him replying with a kiss.

…

Life is a rollercoaster, sometimes you're up, sometimes your down, and sometimes you can't open your eyes for fear of what will hit you next. People come in and share the ride, some get off and leave you to fend for yourself, but once in a lifetime that one person grabs onto those safety railings with you and never let's go.

From the outside, this was just a race. A herd of horses ridden by jockeys dressed in brightly coloured jackets careering down a strip of turf, but to those that knew, it was so much more. It was our redemption, it was our reward, and it was our inheritance for never losing faith, never losing hope and always holding onto that dream, that one day it would be us standing in that winner's circle.

Today wasn't just mine, wasn't just ours, it was his too. Dad was looking down on us smiling and probably shedding a tear or two watching the broken horse and the once broken girl fulfilling their destinies. If you had asked me a year ago if I believed in destiny, if I believed in true love and if I believed that good triumphs over evil, I would have said no to each one. Hope is one thing; faith is another and love is a gift from above. Sometimes they are all we have to cling on to, even when it seems like the whole world is against you, hold onto them and know that whatever happens they will last forever.

Always keep the faith because no matter how hard things get and how impossible the circumstances seem; the sun will always rise in the morning. No matter how long it takes and however many setbacks you face, your time will come, and when it does, it will be so worth it. It may take weeks, it may take months, it may take years, but on a blustery day in the middle of Doncaster the stars aligned, and we took what was ours for the taking.

And now these things remain: faith, hope, and love. But the greatest of these is love.

1 Corinthians 13:13

Beth Smart

Beth moved with her parents to North Yorkshire at the age of four and considers herself to be a true Yorkshire girl. Brought up in the world of horseracing, as the daughter of Group One winning trainer Bryan Smart, she has experienced the immense highs and inevitable lows that are part of the life of a racehorse trainer.

Inspired by the world around her, Beth started writing Racing Hearts in 2017 and has completed her debut novel while studying for a University degree and competing her showjumpers. When not writing or riding, Beth enjoys walking over the moors with her dogs Rosie and Toffee, the inspirations behind Sam the pug.

Playlist

- Let Me Down Slowly – *Alec Benjamin*
- Roundtable Rival – *Lindsey Stirling*
- I Like Me Better – *Lauv*
- Say Something – *A Great Big World*
- Don't Matter – *Lauv*
- Don't Let Me – *Jake Scott*
- Take on the World – *You Me At Six*
- Fight Song – *Rachel Platten*
- I'll Stay – *Riley Clemmons*
- Afire Love – *Ed Sheeran*
- Let's Misbehave – *Cole Porter*
- Young and Beautiful – *Lana del Ray*
- Take Flight – *Lindsey Stirling*
- Look After You – *The Fray*
- Everyone Else – *London Grammar*
- Carry You – *Ruelle*
- Stampede – *Lindsey Stirling*
- Free – *Riley Clemmons*